Bishop's Move

Bishop's Move

COLM KEENA

SOMERVILLE PRESS

Somerville Press Ltd,
Dromore, Bantry,
Co. Cork, Ireland

First published 2013

Designed by Jane Stark
Typeset in Adobe Garamond
seamistgraphics@gmail.com

ISBN: 978-0-9573461-78

Printed and bound in Spain
by GraphyCems, Villatuerta, Navarra

For Helen Clear (1919-2009)

ONE

IN THE BEGINNING, THEN, HE FOUND himself in a penthouse suite, in a lavishly renovated hotel in the centre of the booming city. The enormous room in which he stood spoke of newness, sterility, the hubris of money. Large windows looked out on a park of green grass and red tulips, the modest glow of early lit streetlamps, a flow of traffic beneath a fading Sunday sky. He was not so much tired as wearied on this, what so many considered, his day of glory. It was the spiritual bleakness of his suite that had brought about his sombre, almost tetchy mood; that, and the thought of what was to come.

He sat on the expansive bed, remembering the incense from the mass, how he had lain at the bottom of the altar in a gesture of submission as the floating scent brought him back to the beloved ceremonies of his childhood; how he had struggled to force himself to focus on what was happening and where he was. The sumptuously gowned Archbishop had shared the mass with the other bishops with a practised solemnity. It was an apostolic Church, Whelan had told the congregation with the tone of a pedant. The episcopate was at the core of a two millennia link all the way back to the apostles, to the men who had walked alongside Jesus and heard his words, who had carried his message into human history, from the Holy Land to the entire world. Now Christopher was joining this Apostolic Succession, Whelan had said, making clear the grave and sacred import of what was being done.

For a time, in the midst of the ceremony, Christopher had felt that something momentous was happening. The balsam-scented chrism had moved him greatly. He had been filled with a real and present sense of the history and the divine mission of the Church, and of how he was now part of the most important narrative in human history. But at other times his dominant feeling was a sense of unreality.

He lay back on the softness of the bed and recalled how the organ had filled the church with the sound of Bach, thought again of that sound, the rich product of the great composer's effort to reveal the mind of God. It was a curious mix of joy and logic, an uncanny success; an aural representation of the human spirit and its innate need for the divine. Bach, as Christopher's mother had so often told him, wrote music not as a form of self-expression, but in order to praise God. Therein, he thought now, lay the secret of its power.

Afterwards he had been driven through the city to the hotel. It had become the fashion among those who had amassed riches during the boom years to own a hotel, or hotels, and the hotel to which Christopher was brought was one of the most famous in the country. The amount of money spent on its renovation had sparked a minor scandal, though not outrage. When the hotel had reopened, people had flocked to see it, to revel in paying obscene prices for a modest amount of ordinary wine in an awkwardly large glass. They had flocked to the hotel to stare at the chandeliers and the marble, the besuited staff and abstract art, to wonder how it must feel to be rich beyond measure: and they had left with something to talk about but no insight into the nature of great wealth other than the fact that it allowed for extravagant and wasteful spending.

And it was this lack of existential or spiritual content that struck Christopher as he looked around the room, at the table and two chairs standing isolated between the bed and the end wall, the two large stuffed leather chairs, the low coffee table with its complementary selection of glossy magazines, the modern paintings, the meaning of which, if they had any, eluded him.

The bathroom was almost as large as the bedroom, containing both a bath and a shower, the large tub standing on small lions' paws in the centre of the marble floor. The sink was similarly freestanding. Towels and mirrors and warming rails hung on every wall and the tiles underfoot were pleasantly warm. In the sitting room, which comprised the final element of the suite, there was a sofa and armchairs, a large TV, more paintings, a computer cleverly inserted inside an old mahogany writing desk, a similarly hidden drink-stocked fridge, remote controls that allowed the recessed lights to be brightened or dimmed, the TV to be turned on or off, music to be played loudly or quietly. It was the poverty of its offering that had brought on Christopher's sense of weariness, the glancing, blasphemous thought that where he was to spend the night might be a room where God himself would find it hard to linger.

The time came for him to present himself below, to begin his mission. He washed his face, blessed himself, went out to the corridor and summoned the lift. Two floors down a young, chatting couple got in, noted his black suit and priest's collar with expressions of surprise and ill-disguised resentment, stifled their gaiety, and nodded. The lift descended and they waited for it to set them free. Christopher fingered his new ring, noted the large diamond on the young woman's wedding finger, her accompanying simple gold band. Newly-weds perhaps, he thought, their union recently blessed by a faith they no longer held. The young man's shoes were pointy-toed, a palette smeared brown and cream, made of high quality stiffened leather. When the lift doors opened, the couple breathed with thanks the untainted air, disappeared towards the excited chatter that was coming from the bar.

A woman in a fetching black dress and a boyish haircut smiled openly at him as he walked along the otherwise empty corridor that led to the reception room. He knew her to be the wife of the finance and property expert Michael O'Mahoney, though her name would not come to him. O'Mahoney was more than twenty years older than Christopher. His wife was probably the same age as Christopher, or possibly younger; still in her early forties. She was a beautiful woman who radiated an air of being troubled. He had met such women in the course of his work. Their response to whatever it was that troubled them, he often thought, formed part of whatever it was that made them compelling.

The first time he had seen her he had been ascending the stairs in O'Mahoney's Georgian offices on Merrion Square, six months or so earlier. He had paused when he heard a woman shouting angrily and passionately on the floor above him.

'You just remember how much I know! If you think I don't have the balls to destroy you, to destroy both of us, you are making the biggest mistake you ever made! You bastard!'

A door slammed and she had come thundering down the stairs, her coat open, a red shoulder bag banging against the bannisters behind her. She had passed him as if he was an unseen and unfelt spirit. When, minutes later, O'Mahoney had welcomed Christopher into his spacious office, the businessman had acted as if he had been disturbed from quiet reading.

Now the woman surprised Christopher by giving him her complete attention. She stopped full square in front of him, smiled broadly and touched the collar of his tailored jacket, as if brushing away dandruff, and then, astonishingly, put her hand up and used her palm to rearrange his hair around one ear.

'There,' she said. 'That's better. I like your suit. It sits well on you.'

Somehow her tone acknowledged that she was acting inappropriately.

'You know, of course, that women find power attractive?'

She looked into Christopher's eyes as if they were intimates, smiled wickedly.

'So you'd better be careful.' She lay the same palm flat against his chest.

'Your Grace.'

And then she was gone.

He turned to look after her as she walked away and saw that a younger woman was standing up the corridor, watching. She was a solicitor he knew through his work. Her name was Simone Farrell and she acted for one of the country's top property developers, Bernard or Buzzie Hogan, the owner of the hotel and someone with whom Christopher had dealings. It was obvious she had stopped to observe his encounter with O'Mahoney's wife, and Christopher felt embarrassed when he thought of what she had witnessed. He looked away without acknowledging Simone Farrell or giving her a chance to greet him.

It was only when he had taken a few further steps down the corridor that he remembered O'Mahoney's wife's name: Mary, the same as his mother.

Buzzie Hogan was standing just inside the reception room doors, a glass goblet of white wine clutched in one hand, his other held so the fingertips were gently touching the arm of the Taoiseach, Philip Brady's, blazer. Both tall, imposing figures, Hogan appeared comfortable in his black silk suit while Brady looked as if his opened blazer was too small for him. His bloated belly stuck out, challenging the thread of his shirt buttons. Ever the self-aware politician, Brady caught Christopher's eyes as he entered the room, raised his pint of stout by way of greeting, all the while keeping his head to one side like an attentive confessor as Hogan filled him in on his latest multi-million land deal, or explained to him forcefully how the law needed to be tweaked to promote even greater levels of investment in construction. Why would anyone want to be Taoiseach, thought Christopher.

His mother was on the far side of the room, propped against a windowsill, holding court to an arc of female country cousins dressed as if for a wedding. They were all wearing single-coloured skirt and jacket suits: raspberry; cream; emerald green; Marian blue. His mother, he noted with a surge of affection and pride, was wearing a dignified suit of light brown tweed, a russet silk scarf, and a large silver brooch of a Celtic design. She looked her age: old. She was a thinning cloud of smoke a soft draft would some day soon sweep from the living world.

It was a large room and close to crowded. Most of the people there were strangers to him. When Christopher had expressed surprise at the planned reception, which Buzzie Hogan was paying for, his friend, John, who had been a bishop for some years, had smiled and told him not to worry. The Archbishop's Palace had a list, he had said, 'the fur coat brigade'. Hogan had one too, and that and the fact that the most powerful politician in the State was attending, would ensure that there was an adequate turnout. Ironically, Brady was the only one who looked as if he would rather be anywhere but where he was. Everyone but him appeared to be at ease in their expensive finery, delighted to be in one of the most luxurious hotels in Ireland as the owner's guests, drinking wine that would cost a fortune if it was being consumed in the nearby bar. Brady looked terrified, a simple man trapped in a room full of avaricious property developers and Holy Joes.

Archbishop Whelan was drinking white wine while talking with John in a quiet, episcopal huddle in the middle of the room. A waiter wearing black trousers, a black waistcoat, perfectly shined black shoes and a white shirt with cufflinks was standing beside them holding a tray of drinks. John was exchanging an emptied glass of water for a full one.

'Poland,' the waiter was telling John as Christopher approached.

'Are you a Catholic?' asked Whelan, furrowing his formidable brow in that way that younger priests feared. Despite being in his sixties, he had the physique of the natural soldier, officer class. Whelan governed the Archdiocese in the same imperial way his famous grandfather had ruled over the Free State Army before the Second World War. The Archbishop, Christopher thought, would go to his grave with a flat, muscled stomach, a chest that declared his manhood, and immaculately polished shoes.

'No,' said the waiter. And then, seemingly wanting to be more helpful: 'But when I was very young I was a communist. Both my parents are still communists.'

Whelan made it evident that the waiter was free to go. Christopher joined his fellow bishops, his hands empty, the tray of drinks heading elsewhere. 'So how is the new bishop?' John said by way of inviting him into the conversation. But before Christopher could reply, Whelen interjected, as always oblivious of his rudeness.

'You got the reading wrong.'

Christopher knew that his selection for the position of bishop was due to the fact that a place had suddenly become vacant and that there was no obvious candidate. He had been selected because he was viewed as someone who was reasonably competent and would do no harm. A sense of hurt and defiance had come upon him as he was reading from Luke's Gospel, and he had not finished his selected passage at the appointed spot, but had instead continued: 'For a good tree bringeth not forth corrupt fruit: neither doth a corrupt tree bring forth good fruit. A good man out of the good treasure of his heart bringeth forth that which is good: and an evil man out of the evil treasure of his heart, bringeth forth that which is evil: for of the abundance of his heart, his mouth speaketh.'

Christopher's heart raced as he turned to face Whelan.

'Those words are among my favourite from the Gospels.'

'For crying out loud,' said Whelan, addressing himself to John.

'Discomfiting the comfortable is part of our job,' John replied, smiling at Christopher. When Christopher looked across the room, he saw that his mother was listening to her nieces while watching him. She gave him a nod, as if encouraging him to have courage.

The waiter was passing close by and Christopher thought of raising a hand to make him pause.

'Would you like another drink, Archbishop?'

Whelan was still glowering.

'You can put this on the table for me,' he said, shoving his not yet empty glass forward.

Christopher took the wine glass and leaned down to put it on the low marble-topped table. There were other glasses of wine, some water jugs, a cut-glass vase with an elaborate flower arrangement. People he didn't know were sitting on the heavily stuffed sofa that ran along one side of the table and on the matching armchairs at either end. He got the strong scent of one woman's perfume as he leaned in to put the Archbishop's glass down safely. As he was about to loosen his grip on the glass, a dog's head appeared from a straw bag that was resting on one woman's knees, possibly the knees of the woman with the strong, cloying scent. It was a hairy black and brown terrier and it jerked its head towards Christopher while at the same time emitting a sudden, high-pitched yelp.

The people on the sofa smiled and the woman with the straw bag put her hand under the dog's neck as she prepared to gently scold it. All his life, or at least since puberty, Christopher had had an unwarranted fear of dogs. John had once suggested to him that it was an instance of transference; that perhaps Christopher suppressed his own, natural aggression, and transferred it to dogs, imagining in them the concealed aggression that was stored deep within his soul. This comment from John had been made not as a diagnosis but rather as a conversational tidbit, an instance of the pleasure both he and his best friend took from disinterested observance.

Christopher, in turn, had said that dogs were a cosmic error. The gods had made a beneficent world that was a joy to behold, and had made man mortal so as to intensify the preciousness of the simple fact of being. However an error had occurred. Dogs were a secret passageway to limitless malevolence, portals for the entry of great evil into the world, of horrors so awful that a man might wish that he had never lived.

They had laughed and John had said he did not think such thoughts were appropriate for a Christian. But there was a level at which Christopher had meant what he'd said, and the terrier's aggressive barking caused him considerable, sudden terror. He stumbled as he tried to pull his large, bent-over frame backwards. His hand pushed against the wine glass he had just placed on the table, against a half-filled water jug, and against other wine glasses, knocking them all over. He saw how the faces of the people on the sofa changed so that gentle amusement was replaced by consternation. Through a gap in the crowd he caught a brief glimpse of his mother's puzzled face. His hip hit against an armchair and his body began to fall sideways towards the floor. Even as he was falling, he was thinking: I am falling. I am a six foot four bishop and I am falling to the ground in a crowded room on the day of my consecration, a few feet away from the Taoiseach, surrounded by multimillionaires and their wives and lackeys, and at the very feet of the Archbishop. He effected a silent apology for his inadequacy to his mother, to his departed father. Then his shoulder hit the floor and he rolled so that he ended up lying alongside the blasted table. Whelan had deftly stepped out of his way to let him fall and was directly above him, his face an expression of barely controlled anger but of something else also. He was lank-jawed as the realisation dawned on him that he, and the Church, might have made a monumental error in believing Christopher was a suitable candidate for the episcopate.

The potential truth of that fear pierced Christopher to his core. He lay on the floor to snatch a moment's rest. Water from the toppled jug was flowing across the table, mixing with the spilt wine and dribbling over the edge of the marble so that it fell onto his hand and the finger on which rested his recently blessed bishop's ring.

And something opened within him, at a depth he rarely visited: a determination to rise to the challenge of his new ministry, a conviction that he would not fail.

TWO

IN THE MORNING CHRISTOPHER WOKE and prayed, then washed and
dressed, before taking the lift down to the ground floor where John and
the young public relations executive, Declan Behan, were waiting for
him in the breakfast room. The Archdiocese used Behan for guidance
in its dealings with the media and Christopher had attended a number
of meetings with him over recent months for discussions about the
Bishop Finnegan affair. Although he knew he would be joining them
for breakfast, Christopher's heart sank when he spotted Behan, his
various bits of technology sitting on the breakfast table, his ridiculous
red braces over his Mediterranean blue, white-collared shirt with its
oversized cuffs, the intensity of his ambition so plain for all to see.

Christopher had once attended a meeting in the Archbishop's
Palace where Behan had presumed to take charge, even though it was
attended by the entire archdiocesan episcopate. The fool had even
held something like an electronic clipboard on which he had made
a list of points he thought the bishops, in turn, should emphasise
whenever a journalist put a microphone in front of their lips. Their
message, he had explained to them, mouthing his words slowly as if
English was not his clients' first language, was their message, and all
he wanted to do was to assist them in getting it across. Had it really
come to this, Christopher had thought: a public relations executive
telling the apostolic Church how to convey Christ's message to
humanity? Whelan, he had been sure, had wanted to fling Behan
through a closed window. There were times he felt a sense of kinship
with the Archbishop.

Christopher had been there because the Bishop Finnegan scandal involved bank accounts and money, subjects that were deemed to lie within his field of expertise. A senior figure in the Irish Church with a strong public profile because of his radical work with the poor, Finnegan had been photographed in the Philippines sitting on the terrace of a seaside hotel, wearing nothing but Bermuda shorts and an enormous pair of sunglasses. In front of him on the table was a wine bottle peeping out of a silver ice bucket, and on his lap a young, brown-skinned woman dressed in a pink bikini. The pictures had appeared on the front and inside pages of a Sunday newspaper and the story had sparked a media furore, with radio chat shows and serious current affairs programmes all becoming temporarily obsessed with it.

Each year Finnegan had travelled at his own expense to the Philippines to visit an Irish priest and childhood friend who ran an orphanage there. This was known to the Church. The bishop would spend a week with his friend, but then, unbeknownst both to his friend and to the Church, would spend a further week elsewhere in the archipelago, his priestly clothes in a suitcase, staying in seaside hotels with young local women who were generously paid for their company.

Finnegan had used a credit card during these trips and, at Whelan's insistence, had handed over statements on the account. Christopher had examined them and drafted a report, noting how Finnegan had stayed in top hotels, paid extravagant restaurant bills, and had bought expensive jewellery and other items using the card. At the end of each trip Finnegan had made large cash withdrawals from the credit card account, which Christopher suggested might have been so he could give money to his female companions. A week or so after each trip, the balance on the credit card was paid off with a transfer from an Irish bank, from an account in Finnegan's name. Then the credit card would remain all but unused until the next trip.

When Finnegan was asked to hand over the statements on the bank account used to clear the credit card debts, he at first refused. It was, he said, his personal account and had nothing to do with the Church. Meanwhile the media frenzy was continuing and the Church was trying to hold the line by saying that it was investigating the matter and would, in time, make everything clear. When Whelan warned that he would host a press conference and disclose the position Finnegan was adopting, Finnegan relented and handed over the statements on his bank account. Christopher was asked to examine them. His short report started with what was by far the most important item of information he obtained – the size of the balance on the account. When he produced his report, it caused consternation in the Archbishop's Palace.

A more formal Church inquiry was initiated, with the senior canon lawyer, Dr Reilly, in command. Again Christopher was charged with examining the financial aspects of the affair. The account was seventeen years old and had been opened with a cheque from a solicitor's practice in the west of Ireland, near Finnegan's birthplace. Christopher established that the money had belonged to a client of the solicitor's, a shopkeeper now deceased, who had accumulated a small fortune over the years which she had hidden from the Revenue Commissioners. Afraid in equal measure of the Revenue and the Hereafter, she had asked the solicitor to give it to the Church, and he, in an effort to ensure discretion, had sought to make the donation through Finnegan, with whom the money, as Finnegan himself had put it, 'became stuck'.

Dr Reilly's report was written with great care. The money, he wrote, was an inheritance received by Finnegan which he maintained in his personal accounts and which he used to fund his expenditures in the Philippines. Finnegan's expenditures in the Philippines had not involved one penny from any account belonging to the Archdiocese. Every sentence in the report, in isolation, was truthful, but the entirety constituted a deception. Copies of the report were given to the media, each identifying Reilly's status as a canon lawyer.

Behan was brought in at this stage and told only what was in Reilly's report. When he advised that the Church should tell the whole truth, and not hold anything back, Whelan had turned on him. 'You are not being paid the outrageous fees you are charging so that you can come in here and tell bishops of the Church that they should not lie.' Behan had run a finger around the inside of his starched white collar.

Finnegan was forced to host a press conference on his own where he was questioned about his trips to the Philippines, his sexual relations with a succession of young women, his hypocrisy, and the money. The event was broadcast live on national television. Finnegan held the line that the money was an inheritance that he had received some years ago. When asked the name of the person who had given him such a large sum of money, he said he did not think it would be fair to identify that person. 'She should be allowed rest in peace,' he told the reporter.

'Bishop Finnegan,' asked a young woman reporter who looked to be in her early twenties, 'do you intend to resign?'

The question of Finnegan's resignation had raised the greatest passion within the walls of the Archbishop's Palace. No one had mentioned it until it became the focus of the media coverage. Then Whelan had discussed the matter with the Papal Nuncio. Whelan wanted Finnegan to immediately pen a letter of resignation to the Holy Father. The Papal Nuncio was of the view that bishops of the Church could not be appointed or retired on the basis of what the media felt was appropriate. 'The Church', he had said to Whelan in Latin, 'does not respond to the daily news cycle.' John, who had been present for the exchange, later described it with great glee to Christopher.

Whelan had managed to prevail over the Nuncio. Finnegan, who had engaged his own solicitor at this stage, threatened not to co-operate with the church inquiry if he did not receive an assurance beforehand that he would be allowed to remain in office. Whelan told him that if he did not co-operate with the inquiry, he would call in the Guards, the Revenue Commissioners, tell everything to the media, ensure that Finnegan was sacked by the Pope, and then have him assigned to a parish in Africa. Finnegan had drafted and signed a letter of resignation.

At the press conference Finnegan looked the young woman in the eye and said defiantly: 'One of the first things I did when this scandal started was to offer my resignation to the Holy Father. I feel strongly that he should allow me to resign but will, of course, do whatever it is he instructs me to do.'

In time the Pope accepted Finnegan's resignation and the shell-shocked man was sent to a parish in Sheffield to not only work with the poor, but to live amongst them.

Soon afterwards John had come to see Christopher in his office and told him that the Archdiocese wanted to appoint him in Finnegan's place. 'Your work and your discretion during this whole sorry episode have been noted, and it's been decided you will make a fine bishop,' he said.

And now Christopher was on his way to the national broadcaster, to be interviewed on the most widely heard radio programme on its daily schedule.

After breakfast the three men walked to the hotel car park. Behan was to drive them to the studio. 'Here we are,' said Behan, pulling his keys from his pocket and triggering his car's automatic locking system. The indicator lights glowed orange in the rear of an enormous black Mercedes. Christopher sat in the back and, despite his height, found he had ample leg room. The upholstery was soft white leather that gave an impression of never having been used before. The car purred through the city streets and Christopher noted that at times people stopped and looked at the car to see who might be travelling in such an ostentatious vehicle. A feeling of unease grew ever stronger within Christopher as the journey progressed. As they neared their destination, he broke the silence he had maintained up to then.

'Pull over please. Just pull over here.'

'What's the matter?' John asked.

Christopher was already opening his door. He got out of the Mercedes before answering his friend's question.

'What does it matter what I say on radio if I arrive at the station in a car like this?'

Behan's puffed-up importance seemed to crumple and, for the first time since his consecration, Christopher felt proper, pastoral, concern.

John, as always, understood immediately. When the two bishops were both standing on the pavement, he leaned back into the car and told Behan they would speak with him later. They had pulled over alongside Donnybrook church and John said he knew the way to the back entrance of the radio centre. They walked through a gateway in the low wall to make their way via the church grounds. They walked in silence, Christopher's righteous heart pounding within him.

The bright sun broke through the clouds and its light shone directly onto stained-glass windows depicting the Transfiguration. But the friends walked under the image without noticing.

THREE

AND SO IT CAME THAT CHRISTOPHER found himself in a radio studio, opposite the famous broadcaster Dermot Nolan. The news was on when the producer ushered him into the small room and indicated that he should sit on the opposite side of a round table to Nolan, who stood and shook his hand.

'You're a public figure now,' Nolan said. 'Welcome to the club.'

Christopher couldn't remember a time when he hadn't known of Nolan. His voice and face were familiar, though they had never met before. He could picture Nolan's wife and his family home. He knew his salary and was aware of some commercial buildings in the city in which Nolan's pension fund had an interest. The broadcaster was at one and the same time a complete stranger, and someone Christopher felt he knew.

Behan's view was that Nolan was a consummate professional, with no particular sympathies for the Church, and no antipathy towards it either. From the point of view of the Archbishop's Palace, that was a sentence that required effort to comprehend. Nolan had invited Christopher onto the show because he wanted to introduce him to the general public, but he would also want to revisit the Finnegan case, and get Christopher's views on some other contentious issues on which the media liked to focus when dealing with the Church. Behan suggested that the Church should seek to present Christopher as representative of the new, more open and engaging Church, something Christopher thought sounded like a cliché. A bookkeeper who had spent most of his career alone in his office in the Archbishop's Palace, and who regularly went to visit his elderly mother, he did not think of himself as someone who was anxious to engage. And, anyway, what did the Church do except engage?

Nolan sat, put on his headphones and studied some pages on the table before him. Christopher sat and waited. There was a television screen on the wall behind him, the sound muted, showing a 24-hour news channel. The radio news moved on to the sports report. Nolan would look up every now and then to monitor what was on the TV screen, looking right over Christopher's shoulder but not acknowledging his presence in any way.

Then they were on air.

'Right,' said Nolan, 'welcome back. We have in the studio now the latest member of the Irish episcopate, Christopher Hegarty, appointed to replace Bishop Tom Finnegan whom, as you all know, resigned under a cloud after being photographed in the Philippines with a young, scantily clad woman sitting on his lap in the terrace of an exclusive hotel in a seaside resort. Bishop Hegarty, you are very welcome to the programme.'

Nolan said they would talk in a few minutes about Christopher and his career to date and his views on various issues concerning the Church. 'But first let's deal with the Bishop Finnegan affair, shall we?'

Nolan smiled kindly, holding his stack of A4 pages in front of him. What he would like most, thought Christopher, is my crucifixion. Live on air. A scoop.

'It all starts with the death of someone who left him a bequest, isn't that so?'

Christopher nodded, telling himself it was simply an encouragement to Nolan to continue, but knowing that what he had just done was lie. So much of his work for the Church up to then had been about exposition, accuracy, making matters clear. Telling the truth.

'And Bishop Finnegan told no one about his new-found wealth, placed the money on deposit in an account of his own, and proceeded to treat himself, so to speak, with an annual foreign holiday. Now had he done anything wrong by that stage, in terms of his use of the money?'

Christopher began explaining the rules and conventions covering the personal financial affairs of bishops, the controls that existed over the use of diocesan and parish funds, the history of bishops, and indeed priests, receiving substantial bequests from deceased relatives and parishioners. Nolan seemed fascinated and content, and the subject developed. Christopher noticed that he himself appeared to be operating on automatic pilot. Words were flowing, the script had nothing to do with what Behan had run through with him and, as far as he knew, he was not creating any difficulties for the Archbishop.

Nolan announced an ad break and left Christopher stewing in his seat while he consulted his notes and talked about an upcoming item with his producer. Christopher could see the producer, a woman, and some others, sitting at control panels behind a large pane of glass. John was behind them, sitting with his back against the wall.

It was at this point that Christopher recalled the advice Jesus had given his disciples: 'And when they bring you into synagogues and onto magistrates, and powers, take ye no thought how or what thing ye shall answer, or what ye shall say: for the Holy Ghost shall teach you in the same hour, what you ought to say.'

When they were back on air, Nolan questioned Christopher about his past, where he had grown up, the respective backgrounds of his father and mother.

'So why did you become a priest?'

By this time Christopher was feeling more at ease.

'Actually I don't want to answer that question. It is not because there is any particular mystery, or any matter of contention. It is just that this is a radio programme, and the question you've asked me is quite personal. I think respect for privacy is an important moral exercise.'

'Well, you are here because you have just been made a bishop, to introduce yourself to our listeners.'

Christopher could see Nolan struggle over whether to pursue the topic of intimacy and the mass media, which obviously interested him, or to stick to his script.

'Well we can, I presume, take it that you had a vocation?'

'Yes,' said Christopher. 'And it was also the result of consideration. The Church is a unique institution, a very special opportunity for doing good in the world.'

Nolan began to ask about Christopher's studies at university, his interest in bookkeeping and company law, his work looking after money and other assets, mainly property, held by the Archdiocese.

'It is not what would come into most people's minds when they think of pastoral work, is it?'

Christopher said he liked the work but would grow bored if it was not for the context within which it was carried out. 'I am a servant of the Church, which was established by Christ to be a servant to the people. What greater meaning could anyone's work have?'

'It's not the perspective that was at play when Bishop Finnegan decided to spend the money his old aunt, or whoever, had left him, so that he could have lavish holidays in the Philippines, and pay young ladies for, let us say, their company.'

'Yes, but we must also remember when Christ was in the Temple in Jerusalem, and the scribes and the Pharisees brought in the woman who had been caught in the act of adultery, so they could test him. They said the law of Moses prescribed that she should be stoned. And he stooped down and began to write with one finger in the dust on the ground, as if he hadn't heard them. And when they persisted, he said: "He that is without sin among you, let him first cast a stone at her." And then he stooped back down, and one by one they walked away, beginning with the eldest until, in the end, it was just the woman and Jesus, who was again writing with a finger in the dust on the floor. And when he looked up and saw they were all gone, he noted that none of them had condemned her, and said that he did not condemn her either.'

'But the Church viewed Bishop Finnegan's actions as unacceptable, or otherwise it would not have accepted his resignation.'

'Yes,' said Christopher, 'but there was of course a lot more to the whole affair than the brief summary you gave at the outset of this interview.'

Nolan froze. His focus zeroed in on Christopher in a way it had not done before. Christopher fought against the impulse to panic. He recalled the principle he used when drafting complex reports: make a statement, review its veracity and, if you are satisfied, proceed.

'Can you tell us what you are referring to?'

'Yes I can.'

Nolan, consummate professional that he was, had the good sense to stay quiet and let Christopher be the next to speak.

Bishop Finnegan, Christopher said, had received money from a solicitor who was acting for the estate of an elderly woman who had left the money to the Church. She was not a relative. The money was at all times intended for the Church, not for Bishop Finnegan.

'Furthermore, my understanding is that the money had been accumulated over a number of decades, and was income that had not been declared to the Revenue Commissioners. It had been kept in an account of an Irish bank in Jersey. The money is associated with what on the face of things appears to have been a succession of potentially criminal acts. So you can see why the Church found this unacceptable. For Bishop Finnegan to have remained in his position would have involved the Church being guilty of the type of hypocrisy that so annoyed Jesus.'

Nolan struggled to suppress his excitement. 'Let's take this slowly,' he said.

Christopher refused to identify the solicitor or the woman who had bequeathed the money, but otherwise he spoke as clearly and as openly as he could. There was no break for advertisements as Nolan sought to shine light on as many corners of the story as possible. When he asked if the Reilly report was not an effort by the Church to mislead, Christopher said he had felt unhappy about how it had been worded.

'Beyond that, you will have to ask Dr Reilly, the sole author of the report.'

Nolan asked if the Garda Síochána had been informed of what the Church had discovered.

'I don't know,' said Christopher, 'but I think there is a strong argument that they should be told. Likewise, the Revenue Commissioners. The money given to Bishop Finnegan should really be used to settle any outstanding tax bills that exist.'

'But if Bishop Finnegan was given the money, a lot of money, so he could pass it on to the Church, and he kept it and spent it himself, that's stealing. Simple, straightforward theft. A crime that every child understands.'

'Yes,' said Christopher. 'That is how I see it. Of course Bishop Finnegan is not here to defend himself, but that is my understanding of how matters stand.'

Nolan said the programme was coming to an end, and had run over time. He apologised, on air, to the newsreader, who was somewhere else in the radio building. When the newsreader began to read out the headlines, the first item was the fact that Christopher had said that the money spent by Bishop Finnegan had been intended for the Church, and that he, Christopher, felt the Garda and the Revenue should investigate the affair.

'A spokesman for the Archdiocese,' the newsreader continued, 'said it had no comment to make but would be issuing a comprehensive statement in the near future.'

Christopher left the studio and joined John out by the producers' control panels. His friend raised his left eyebrow in a discreet expression of inquisition. 'They've called a taxi for us,' John said, and he showed Christopher a yellow docket one of the staff had given him.

In the taxi they told the driver to take them to the Archbishop's Palace in Drumcondra. The car was entering Donnybrook village when Christopher's mobile phone rang. It was Whelan.

'What the hell have you just done? What type of game do you think you're playing?'

'What was I supposed to do? He asked and I told him.'

'He didn't bloody well ask! You offered the information, *and* your bloody opinions. You practically called for Finnegan to be jailed! And you made me and the whole Archdiocese look like liars.'

'If I had let him conduct the interview on the basis that the picture created by the Reilly report was a true picture, then I would have been misleading him and the listeners.'

'You never said anything about this before.'

'I wasn't asked.'

'Oh, for God's sake, man! You're a bloody bishop now, more's the pity. You can't be staying silent in here and then going shouting your mouth off in the outside world!'

Christopher's heart was thumping violently inside his chest.

'I didn't want to lie.'

'It's not as simple as that. The Nuncio wanted us to proceed on the basis of Reilly's report. Do you understand what I'm telling you? And what you've just done?'

'I did what was right,' Christopher said, surprising himself with his tone.

'The Nuncio will think I put you up to it,' Whelan said. 'Stay away from me. I don't want to see you for a week at least. Turn off your mobile phone. If you speak to any journalists, I'll send you to Timbuktu. And you are not to tell them that I told you not to speak to them! Do you understand?'

Whelan hung up before Christopher could respond.

John did not need to be told what Whelan's reaction to the radio interview had been.

'He wanted to be more open about it,' John said, 'but the Nuncio overruled him and made him stick to the Reilly report. The Archbishop is a tyrant but he's a good man.'

Christopher asked the taxi driver to take him to Broadstone. No one spoke for a while other than the taxi man, who muttered occasional abuse at the drivers of other vehicles.

'Do you have anything against Finnegan?' John asked as they were crossing the Liffey.

'No. He's an egomaniac but there's no taking from the good work he's done.'

John chuckled.

'He won't be happy with you. He'll think you were out to get him, or that Whelan is behind all this.'

Christopher said that the words people utter had to stand for something. 'We learn that Finnegan stole a load of money that was in turn stolen from the State and we cover it up because we know him and because he's a bishop. It nullifies everything we say. It makes us stand for nothing.'

'There are ways of dealing with such issues.'

They were being driven alongside the Black Church. When he was a child, Christopher was told that if you circled it twelve times at midnight, you met the Devil.

'If an Irish bishop goes to jail for stealing from the Church, it will make headlines around the world. Do huge reputational damage.'

'Maybe not,' said Christopher. 'If the Church does everything it can to assist any inquiry, and makes it clear that it believes its bishops should be treated before the law in the same way as everyone else, people will respect that.'

The car stopped in a narrow street of yellow-bricked terraced houses, beside the primrose-coloured door of the house where Christopher lived. Mrs Lacey, his elderly neighbour, was standing in her doorway, smoking. Christopher kept the door closed while John spoke.

'You know Whelan asked me a lot of questions about you before it was decided to make you a bishop. I told him that you were honest, principled, loyal, able and straight. But maybe there are other aspects to your character that you've been hiding all these years.'

John said he would phone Christopher that evening and update him on events. When Christopher got out of the car, Mrs Lacey was stamping on the butt of her cigarette.

'I heard you on the radio,' she said. 'Fair dues. You've set the cat among the pigeons now!'

FOUR

AFTER THESE THINGS, IT HAPPENED THAT Christopher found himself in the short hallway of his two-bedroomed terraced home. An old wooden door, as old as the house itself, gave onto the small front room in which there was an attractive tin fireplace, a sofa, shelves on each side of the fireplace, and a music system. The window in the room looked directly onto the footpath outside so that when people walked by, Christopher heard their conversation as they approached and as they walked away. Despite the fact that it was such a small room, north-facing, with walls that were painted dark brown, it was his favourite place in the house. On many evenings, especially in the winter, he would close the door, pull the curtains, and lie on the sofa in the lamp-lit room, listening to music. Bach's *Goldberg Variations*, Glenn Gould's murmurings an audible accompaniment as he played. Or Pablo Casals' performance in the White House for President Kennedy, his musical groans also audible. Or Debussy's *Six Epigraphes Antiques*. Or, at times, the *German Requiem*, by Brahms, with the beautiful singing of Kiri Te Kanawa, though he felt uncertain about being moved by a work written by the composer at the time of his mother's death when his own mother was still alive, and also because of the work's determined omission of Jesus' death as a source of comfort and redemption.

On occasion he lit a fire and took comfort from the light and heat coming from the small hearth. Sometimes too, and more often in recent years than heretofore, he would drink wine while he listened and relish the way it and the music worked together on his senses. It had become a secret refuge for him, a private realm he could think of during his days and look forward to. Some nights he would make a number of trips to the kitchen to refill his wineglass, even though it was a capacious one. Sometimes he brought the wine bottle with him from the kitchen and, more than once, when he had sought to rise from the sofa at his evening's end, he had difficulty doing so. One night he all but finished a second bottle while listening to Rachmaninov's beautiful Vespers and had to crawl up to bed, laughing quietly least Mrs Lacey should hear him through the wall and wonder had he gone mad.

Another original door at the end of the short hall gave into the least satisfactory room in the house. A wooden stairs, the steps of which were of inadequate depth, led to the two upstairs rooms. A door diagonally across the room gave onto to the flat-roofed extension, in which there was a small bathroom and a tiny kitchen. He had given up trying to make the room hospitable, and used it as both a dining room and an office. A work station was set up against one wall, and a small table and two chairs against the wall opposite. In his years in the house he had never shared a meal.

The kitchen was small. Its windows were south-facing and he could stand in one spot and chop vegetables, fetch what he wanted from the fridge, reach the presses where he kept his pots and pans and oils, and turn and operate the cooker. He could also, as he worked on a spring or a summer's evening, see out to the yard which had been built by the home's previous owner.

The houses had been constructed with Ringsend brick, a distinctively yellow brick no longer manufactured. When Mrs Lacey had her back wall knocked down for her extension, the occupant of Christopher's house had asked for the bricks, and had used them to pave her small yard and also to cover its walls. There was a small flowerbed alongside the wall that divided the tiny yard from Mrs Lacey's, and a magnificent rose bush grew there. Each spring and summer it produced hundreds of pink flowers, and Christopher had learned to cut off the heads when they shed their petals, so that the bush continued to produce new blooms. Every winter he treated it to a bag of farmer's manure as part of his covenant with this plant which brought him so much pleasure.

The woman who had owned the house had died in the yard, the victim of a sudden and unforeseen aneurysm. Her pious and heartbroken mother had left what was then a small, cheap house, in a poor, unpopular neighbourhood, to the Church. Since then, the country had become transfixed by one of the most sustained and spectacular property booms in postwar Europe, and the small, terraced house was now considered to be an attractive property in a central location. It would fetch ten or perhaps fifteen times the average industrial wage if placed on the market, and was the type of house sought by young, upwardly mobile professionals.

Christopher had a small music player in the kitchen, and he would listen to music while cooking and often drink a glass of white wine while doing so. If it was a warm evening he might eat by the open door to the yard, and sit there afterwards, listening to music and sipping a last glass of red, underneath the city's sky, away from the noise and the crowds. He might have been a hermit in the desert such were the moments of peace he experienced.

He slept in the back bedroom because it was away from the noise of the street (though in truth there was little noise) and because it was south-facing. The houses backing onto his yard were terraced cottages, and because his road was on the crest of a hill, the view from his window was unimpeded all the way across the city to the Wicklow mountains. The view was of slate rooftops, church spires and an infestation of cranes.

The upstairs room to the front of the house ran its whole width and had the potential to be the nicest room in the building, but he had never developed any use for it other than for keeping his clothes in the wardrobe and the chest of drawers there, and for dumping those objects that had made their way into the house for which he had no, or only infrequent, need.

Christopher had been in many priests' and bishops' houses over the years and noted their cold, masculine, utilitarian interiors, or their overdone, feminine, housekeepers' efforts to make them into homes.

John's was his favourite, in part because it was filled with books and other exterior evidence of the interior life lived, but mostly because of the gardens, front and back, where his slightly older friend nurtured flowerbeds, fruit trees and even small, yearly crops of potatoes, tomatoes and beetroots. Every September John would be full of the joys of his beetroots, which he liked to juice with apple, carrot, and some ginger root. 'Sets you up for the winter,' he would say. 'Makes you invincible.'

John's house was a rather grand, three-bedroom redbrick, in a quiet suburb close to the Archbishop's Palace. A woman came and cleaned it twice a week, and made the occasional, decorative addition, but there was no denying the fact that the house was home to a childless man who lived alone. It was a place where a man could sleep at night, eat his meals out of the wind, wash and change his clothes; read on into the early hours while the less lonesome slept in the houses around him.

John did not drink alcohol. He disapproved of Christopher's interest in rich food washed down with good wine, of his tendency to speak with enthusiasm about such matters. 'Gluttony is a sin,' he would say lightheartedly, to which Christopher would reply: 'So too is your veneration of your beetroots, and your excessive admiration for the beneficial effects of root ginger on the intestines. Your interest in your health is a form of vanity.'

John rose early in the mornings, put on unsightly black latex pants, and ran for miles around the still sleeping streets of Drumcondra, Glasnevin and Phibsborough. He was so aware of his energy and fitness that he sat on the edges of chairs, anxious at all times to be up and active, making use of his beloved, well-tended, God-given body.

Christopher walked through his house to the kitchen, opened the door to the yard, and sat there looking out at the roofs of the cottages opposite. He had not wanted to be made a bishop. He could see with great clarity now that what he had not wanted was the responsibility of management. And the reason he had not wanted that was, simply, because it involved choices, often difficult choices, and he did not think he was good at evaluating complex human situations, or coping with the emotional tension that compromise involved. He liked accountancy and company law precisely because of their logic and rules, because they allowed him to inhabit a virtual world where choices could be made which were demonstrably correct. In the sphere of human organisation, the choices you made could not be shown to be correct.

And so, he thought, sitting on his chair looking out at the cloud-strewn sky, it was his practice to try to stick to clear principles. He had been asked a question, and he had told the truth. He had cleared up a falsehood. The people had a right to know. A serious crime may have been committed. The authorities should investigate. It was a moral tenet known to a child: tell the truth and shame the Devil.

Certainty brought on a burst of emotion and an irrepressible impulse to stand. Bugger Whelan and the Papal Nuncio, he thought. And the Vatican. He wasn't going to tell lies. Let the consequences be whatever they would be.

After pacing the yard for a bit, he went into the house to call his mother from the phone in the hall. When she answered, he said he would call on her in about an hour, and asked if there was anything he should bring.

Yes, she said. A half-dozen eggs, preferably small or medium-sized.

'I was on the radio,' he said.

'Oh yes. I heard that,' she replied.

And she hung up.

FIVE

Up at the Phibsborough shopping centre Christopher sat on the low wall beside the bus shelter. The sky was a mix of light blue and grey, the low silver sun behind the thin cloud something to behold. There were others waiting with him, including three noisy youths in cheap tracksuits whom he presumed should have been at school but were instead smoking cigarettes and conducting a foul-mouthed conversation. Theirs, he thought, is a lack of wisdom rather than a moral failing. Each 'fuck', 'bollix', 'cunt' they uttered was another coarsening of their interior selves, their souls, as was the fact that they were not at school, learning patience, respect for their teachers, the effect of the Gulf Stream on the climate in which they would live their lives. If asked, they would no doubt blame their relative material deprivation for the self-defeating attitudes they had adopted towards the world. He wondered if they were ignorant of the supreme importance of motive and the inner life; of how the ceaseless flow of choices that each person made influenced future choices and made people what they were ceaselessly becoming. He felt a desire to help these young men but also an acceptance that he could not directly do so.

After boarding the bus he was collecting his ticket from the driver when one of the young men, already on the bus, turned and pulled his tracksuit pants down, showing his bare bottom to some young women still standing at the bus stop. 'Kiss that!' the young man shouted. He and his colleagues erupted into loud, carefree laughter and pushed against each other as they clambered up the stairs. The last one to begin climbing shouted up at the young man who had bared his bottom; 'You're fucking evil, you are!'

Christopher sat downstairs, at a seat that allowed him to stretch his legs. He spent his journey, along with the others on the bus, listening to the loud, foul-mouthed and inane conversation of the young men on the upper deck, thankful to them for the way their noise and nonsense provided a distraction from the ideas that were troubling him.

He had not, in his priestly career, had much experience of evil. Once, in a strange incident, he had visited the large, somehow bare home of a middle-class family whose father he had just buried. They gave him sandwiches and tea, and the woman and her grown children had sat with him in the kitchen discussing their grief, the life of the man who had died, but also other, less spiritual, aspects of their lives, such as their sporting activities, and their vocational prospects and ambitions. In time he found himself becoming troubled by something he sensed about the family, a combination of intensity and emotional paucity, and when at one stage he excused himself and went to the toilet, he found himself, quite unexpectedly, convinced that he was in the presence of evil. It was as if the house was drenched in malevolence, in the way, perhaps, that rising damp could find its way into every wall in a building, making its presence part of the atmosphere in every room. He did not know whether the evil spirit of the place was connected in some way with the life of the man over whose burial he had just officiated, though the thought did for some reason fix itself in his mind. What struck him most forcefully was how convinced he was of the presence of evil, and of how it seemed so strongly to him, against all his philosophical and religious beliefs, to be located in the stuff of the house he was in. He felt fear, almost to panic, but he did not succumb to it and he returned to the grieving family in the kitchen, to more ham sandwiches and tea, and their evident goodwill. He spent some more time keeping them company, contributing to the comfort of conversation, while all the time feeling in his bones his recent encounter with the extra-corporeal malevolence that he felt haunted the house.

The bus stopped at the traffic lights at the top of St Mobhi Road. When it started again, it turned towards Glasnevin village. Glimpsing the gates to the Botanical Gardens up ahead, Christopher decided he would go for a quick walk there in the hope that it would change his mood and the nature of his thinking. He pressed the bell that was on a pole beside him and the driver pulled the vehicle to a halt at the stop beside the gated entrance. He thanked the man as he alighted from the bus and, for the first time since getting up, felt a surge of gratitude for the day's beauty, for the crispness of the invigorating air.

A gardener from America with whom he was friendly, James, was sitting in the guardian's hut a few metres inside the gate, and he waved warmly at Christopher as he saw him enter. This too contributed to Christopher's growing sense of the goodness of the world, and the blessed nature of being.

'Hiya, Christopher. Heard you on the radio. Way to go.'

Christopher went and stood by the open window to the hut, noting as he did so how the energy and strength of the young man's greeting contributed to the lifting of his mood.

'I'm in a bit of bother,' Christopher said.

'I'd say you are. Jesus! It's all over the news. Everyone's going crazy. They've been over to England already, where is it, Sheffield, knocking on the door of that guy Finnegan. They've been talking about you in the Dáil, for God's sake. You're on the historical record! The opposition has been questioning the Taoiseach. Brady said it was a matter for the Archdiocese. You can tell he doesn't want to know – it's got nothing to do with me. But you know all this! Who am I telling?'

'Actually I don't know what's going on. I went on Nolan's radio programme and I haven't heard anything since.'

'Ah man! You're the top item on the news, and everyone is talking about you on all the chat shows. Jesus, half the people who've come into the gardens this morning have stopped to talk about you.'

'What are they saying?'

'Well, saving your presence, but they think Finnegan is a low life who should be in jail. And they are being pretty hard on the Archbishop, and on your canon lawyer – what's his name, Reilly. He's getting a lot of stick. Pretty much the same for the Archbishop. They're even giving out about the Pope! But not you. You're a hero. You're the saviour! The only guy everyone feels can be trusted.'

Christopher said he thought he'd better keep his head down for a while. James gave him that beaming open smile that made him such a popular figure.

'So, I mean, what did you do it for? Did you mean to? You've got something against that Finnegan guy, right?'

Christopher said he had nothing against Bishop Finnegan, and even admired the work he had done for the poor. He just thought people should try to tell the truth. 'It makes life a lot simpler.'

'Well, in this instance, I think you're one hundred per cent wrong there! One thing you can say about the shit you're in now is, it's not simple.'

James laughed out loud as he said this and Christopher, infected by his good cheer, laughed with him. The oppression he had been feeling was by now entirely vanquished. He left James and set out on his walk, passing as he did so the leaf-shaped restaurant building through the windows of which he could see retired people and middle-aged mothers drinking coffee and chatting. Some of them waved at him as he passed, while others nudged or nodded to the people they were with, to bring to their attention the fact of his presence. He was in the media, a feature of the public life of the day, and this in itself attracted attention.

It was something he had noted upon becoming a priest. The distinctive clothes and Roman collar made him a public figure, with less right to privacy than a lay person. As John had put it to him, he was not his own property any longer. Once his elevation to the position of bishop had been announced, the public's interest in him had increased yet again. He was a public personality, even before this latest controversy concerning Finnegan's money. 'People want to belong to something greater than themselves, and we supply a way of being that' was how John had put it.

Christopher had wondered too about the link between this need people had, and power. Philip Brady was a frequent visitor to the

Botanical Gardens, especially on Sunday mornings when he came with his wife and five children. People were excited by the mere presence of the Taoiseach, were delighted and energised when they received his attention. Powerful people such as Brady walked through life capable of dispensing cheerfulness simply through a wave of the hand, the bestowal of a smile, the sacrifice of a few minutes' idle chatter.

It was a phenomenon Brady had used for personal advantage. He roamed the country so as to have, literally, hundreds of brief, chance encounters every week with members of the public who would thereafter speak fondly of him and spread the myth of his ordinariness and good nature. Brady had associated himself with the country's sudden and unexpected upturn in its economic fortunes, and these handshakes and brief exchanges about sport and the weather became a medium through which the population could express its delight with how matters had turned out. And at each election Brady got his reward, his popularity soaring to heights other politicians did not allow themselves to dream of.

Christopher walked along by the walls of Glasnevin Cemetery thinking about fame and political position. Jesus, he recalled, had been tempted by the Devil to use his divine nature to experience the attractions of earthly power. Everything, as the Chinese apparently believed, had its two sides, its dual nature. Christopher's role in the Church allowed him to boost people's spirits as he walked about the city. All he had to do was to pause and share a few words with people as they passed, and he contributed to the amount of good cheer in the world. And this, of course, could serve to make him vain, pompous, self-important, a less successful man, priest and bishop. Traps lay everywhere.

As Christopher was nearing the entrance to the walled garden, he saw coming towards him an elderly couple with whom he had a nodding acquaintance. The woman was wearing a vivid yellow tracksuit while her husband's was a startling blue. Both had on spotless white running shoes and Christopher couldn't help thinking that their every possession was most probably immaculate. They were walking at speed, their arms pumping, and when they came upon him they jolted to a halt.

'Good morning, your Grace.'

'My name's still Christopher,' he said, and everyone laughed.

'You can hear the wailing and gnashing of teeth from the Archbishop's Palace,' the man said.

'Lucky for me,' said Christopher, 'that I have the Botanical Gardens to hide in.'

'Well, I think you were damned right,' said the woman. Her face was half-covered by her reflector sunglasses. 'Fair's fair. What that man did was disgraceful. Going with prostitutes over in the Philippines and then coming back here so we can all praise him for his work with the poor. It's disgusting.'

Christopher thought again of Christ's response when the woman caught in the act of adultery had been brought before him. The Gospels were silent as to what Jesus had written with his fingertip on the sand of the temple floor. It was the only instance in the Gospels of Jesus writing, and there was no mention of his ever reading anything.

'The law should be the same for everyone,' he said, hoping this would not add to any feelings of rancour or wrath the woman was harbouring.

'Exactly,' said the woman. 'You were perfectly right to speak out. There's a lot more have done worse and that are still swanning around, lording it over the rest of us. Wasn't it hypocrisy that used to make Christ himself angry? Well, it makes my blood boil too.'

Christopher waited a moment before making his next comment.

'It's a beautiful day for a walk. Aren't we blessed to have this place?'

'Aren't we just,' the woman said, her mood changing with the speed of a cloud's shadow. 'I often say to Martin, this place is one of the best-kept secrets in Dublin.'

'Long may it remain so,' said Christopher, and with that they parted.

Inside the walled garden he had paused to examine a row of cabbages when one of the workers came to a halt beside him.

'So,' he said, 'will Whelan have to go?'

It was Arnold, a tall man with close-cropped hair and narrow eyes that were prone to being bloodshot. James had told him once of how Arnold, in an apparent fit of existential frustration, had disappeared for two months, leaving home and family and work without any notice save a note he left for his wife telling her he loved her, was going away for a while, was not having an affair, and was not in the least suicidal. 'I just need some time out,' he had said. When he had reappeared, he had asked that no one ask him where he had been or what it was that had happened to him, and in time he had been allowed back into the life that had formerly, it seemed, caused him so much anguish but to which he now wanted to return.

'I hope not, Arnold,' said Christopher. 'The Archbishop is a good man, doing a difficult job at a difficult time. He's doing his best, believe me.'

'I'd say the Vatican is sticking its nose in.'

The small apple trees, Christopher noticed with a sense of assuaged guilt, were as miserable and unhealthy-looking at those in his mother's side garden.

'I'd better not say anything about that,' Christopher said.

They both laughed as if there was no need to say anything further.

'Nothing's ever simple,' Christopher said.

'You're right there,' said Arnold. 'Spot on. I could tell you stories about this place that would make your hair stand on end. Management is always management, no matter what organisation you're talking about.'

It was their habit to stand alongside each other during their brief exchanges, looking off into the distance at the inadequacies of the world.

'The thing is, though, you've embarrassed them in public. That's what you have to remember, Christopher. Everything is about status. You've caused them to lose face and they hate that. I'd watch out if I were you.'

SIX

So CHRISTOPHER WENT TO THE HOUSE where his mother lived and where he had lived as a boy and as a young man. He used his own key and when he opened the door he could see down the hall through to the kitchen, and again through the open back door to the small yard where his mother was lying in her easy chair, in the sunlight, covered with two thick wool blankets, one of his father's old caps on her head, her eyes closed. Music he knew from his childhood, a clarinet and viola double concerto by Bruch, was coming from the CD player in the kitchen.

She did not hear him opening the front door, nor sense his presence in the hallway. Perhaps, he thought, she is dead. One day it would be so, and he would find her in some moment just like this, in a room in the house, her music playing unheard from her music system or the radio, she lying as if in repose, the house filled with sunlight, or the peace of evening, her spirit gone from her body. His mother whom he loved lost to him for ever.

He closed the door loudly, so that his coming upon her in the yard would not startle her, and also, perhaps, to see if she would stir, to confirm, or dispel, his worst fear. She did not move, so he walked loudly down the parquet floor of the hall, and stomped down the steps to the kitchen.

'Mammy.'

He turned down the music until it was barely audible. She opened her eyes, addressed him while looking at the blue of the heavens.

'Ah, there he is. The man who's causing all the bother.'

The remains of her lunch were on the kitchen table. A soup bowl, a glass that had held milk. Tinned soup probably. One of the ways her advanced age manifested itself was a developing aversion to food. Not only did she eat less, the presence of any quantity of food in the house had become unpleasant to her. He rarely ended a visit without being given something to take away: a few apples; milk she didn't want; some tubs of yoghurt. Meanwhile she grew lighter and smaller by the week, so that he thought she would leave him not by dying so much as by progressively fading until she eventually vanished.

'Why don't you bring a chair out here? It's a lovely day. Make yourself some tea if you want. I'll have some too.'

The house was more than a century old. It was semi-detached and beyond it and its partner house there was a terrace of the same age. A laneway came in from the road, alongside the triangular garden to the side of house, past the high metal gate into the backyard, and then along behind the terrace. Each house in the terrace had a plot of land directly behind it, on the other side of the lane, where the residents had once parked their horses. Some of the plots were quite large, as big as a small field, but attempts by some neighbours to get planning permission to build had been stymied by problems with access. 'Thank God for small mercies,' his mother had said.

It was in the largest of those plots, at the farthest end of the lane, that an event which contributed to his becoming a priest had occurred. A strange event difficult to put into words, which he had declined to describe when being interviewed that morning by Nolan.

As a boy, the lane had seemed to him to be enormous. Down in the plots he and his friends had imagined themselves to be Cowboys and Indians circling each other on the Great Plains, or Robin Hood and his Merry Men, masters of Sherwood Forest, or Custer and his soldiers on their way to their Last Stand. Their dreams had come from the English comic books they had read, the American films and programmes they had watched on television and in the cinema.

Yet his childhood had also included the last echoes of an Irish Republic where the Church considered itself superior in temporal power and legitimacy to the government. His father had told him a story about his Aunt Catriona, who had become a nun and gone behind convent walls in England, expecting never to be seen again, but had then been released by the changes introduced by the Second Vatican Council. While in Dublin on a short holiday home, she had been refused permission by the then Archbishop to stay in her brother's home, and told instead to spend her nights in a convent. One evening when she was walking down Griffith Avenue, she was spotted by the Archbishop, who was being driven along in his large black Citroën. The car pulled over and the Archbishop stepped out to roundly scold her for still being outside after the six o'clock curfew he had arbitrarily imposed on visiting nuns.

His attitude towards the Archdiocese was like that of an absolute monarch, his father had said to Christopher, with a tone of disapproval that had made a lasting impact.

Christopher could not remember the Corpus Christi parades that had passed along his street, the houses bedecked in papal bunting, the frocked priests shepherding the golden monstrance that held the sacred host, but his parents did have a photograph of him in his buggy on the pavement on the day of one such parade. He could remember Lenten periods when the whole neighbourhood left their homes at almost the same time to attend weekday evening mass in the local church. When during benediction he had bowed his head in the incense-filled church, there were no boundaries between the security he had felt because of his parents' love, the security he had felt because of the presumed goodness of his neighbours, and the security he had felt because of God's omniscience and love.

Then it had all collapsed. Now he said mass on weekday mornings to thin congregations who attended with the aid of Zimmer frames, walking sticks, and wheelchairs. The young people who came to church tended to be Poles, Lithuanians or Hungarians. The young women who came to the altar to receive communion included African or Filipino nurses from the local hospital, and he would look down at the submission and trust on their beautiful faces as they closed their eyes and opened their white-palmed hands to receive, and wonder at how times had changed.

He prepared tea and some slices of carrot cake, brought them out to the yard and placed them on the small table, sat on the kitchen chair he had fetched for himself.

'Are you in trouble?' she asked, allowing herself a chortle. She had a way of talking that made people feel she found their difficulties amusing. Her music students used to have a wary respect for her, and few who lasted were cavalier about their homework. She was always kindest to the girls.

'I have been told to stay away.'

'I have no sympathy for that Finnegan,' she said. 'I wouldn't begrudge him a few euro and a few nights in a good hotel, and God knows he deserved the occasional holiday, but taking advantage of those poor young women. If he didn't like being celibate, he could have had a secret wife, like the priests in Africa. But the poor young women, having to be with a old man like him. Men can be right pigs.'

He told her the Archbishop had called him after the radio interview and had chewed his ear off.

'I'm sure he did,' she said, delighted. 'He's in a right corner now.' She sat back in her chair and let out a short laugh. 'God but can't people be awful stupid.'

When he asked her how she was, she told him she was old.

'Did you know what you were doing?' she asked.

He said he probably did.

'You were always a funny child. Quiet as a mouse; pretending to be as biddable as they come, yet always going your own way. Lots of people made the mistake of thinking that just because you were quiet and polite, you were a pushover. Looks like the Archdiocese has done just that now. Ah God, I hope I'm around long enough to see the end of this one.'

When the time came to go into the house, he helped her to stand by putting one hand under her right arm. Once again he was shocked by her insubstantiality. She paused when she stood, said she sometimes felt dizzy. She was wearing grey woollen socks over dark brown tights, and small, laced brown shoes. He kept hold of her arm until she had climbed the two steps into the kitchen, then went back to clear up the yard. She had not touched the cake.

'The lightbulb in the dining room needs to be changed. Could you do that? You'll find one under the stairs.'

He did as he had been asked. The extent to which she had come to depend on him had increased steadily over the years and become a way of communicating their mutual affection. In more recent times she had grown more open, less diffident about her dependency. His nearness and availability had become one of the pleasures in her life, and her increasing frailty had become a medium through which she could allow him express his love.

He found a bulb and replaced the one that was no longer working. On the way back, he stopped to review the cracks in the arch in the hallway, where the exterior wall was straining to pull away from the house, which had settled awkwardly over the years.

His father had responded to the effects of the house's movement by taping over the cracks, and then painting over the tape. Christopher had more recently offered to fill the cracks with plaster but his mother had laughed, and said he would probably end up knocking down the house. When he had suggested getting workmen to do it, she had dismissed the idea.

'Why bother? They would charge a fortune and probably make a hames of it. I'll be gone before it falls down. Let whoever gets the house after me bother with it.'

In her will she had instructed that the house be sold and that he be given twenty per cent of the proceeds. Another thirty per cent was to be divided amongst her various nieces and nephews in County Westmeath. The rest was to go to the Church. At the time she made the will, his percentage would have amounted to a few tens of thousands, but these days it would be a six-figure sum.

Some young family would move in, have builders strip the house to the bone, remove every vestige of the lives Christopher and his parents had lived there. They would level the uneven floor in the kitchen, might even knock down the whole return and build a modern extension. But time would pass and the house would become inhabited by the ghosts of their days. Just as the house was inhabited now by the ghost of Christopher's youth; the leavings of his mother in her prime; the buried sound of her music classes; by the quiet of his father's spirit; by Christopher's memories of him in his favourite chair by the window in the front room, the standard lamp illuminating the pages of his book, his eyes closed as he enjoyed yet another stolen snooze.

Christopher told his mother that he had been down at the Botanical Gardens, and asked if she would like to go for a short walk. She said she had been to mass that morning, and that was enough walking for her these days. When she came back, she had wanted to do nothing other than to lie on her easy chair in the yard and sleep.

'But you know what happened? That young girl up the road, in the old Deasy house, started to practice her viola. She's a good little thing. She practises every day, and she's coming along. She was playing Gounod's *Sérénade*, do you remember that? I used to teach it to my students. She played it well, though a bit too fast. I was half-tempted to go up the road and give her a few pointers. Then, when she had finished, I went inside and I opened the piano. I don't know why I tried to play; my fingers aren't up to it any more.'

So, instead, she had put the Bruch concerto on the CD player in the kitchen, turned up the volume and left the back door open, in the hope that the girl up the terrace might hear and take it as encouragement.

'She's a lovely girl. It would cheer you up just to see her. On Saturday I met her and her two young brothers in the shop, buying sweets, involved in intense discussions about what they would buy, and whether they would share. You know the little lad with the red curls, and the blond one, who wears the football shirts? It was cold but they were wearing flip-flops. I let some money fall and the three of them immediately leaned down to pick it up for me. Then, when I was walking back up the hill and they caught up with me, the girl stopped and offered me a sweet. When I took one, the two boys felt compelled to offer me ones too. I took a sweet from each of them and then they hurried off up the hill. God, I love seeing them run. They do my heart good.'

SEVEN

LATER THEY WERE IN THE FRONT ROOM, watching the six o'clock news. It showed footage of Christopher's ordination mass, of the house in Sheffield where Finnegan now lived, of Whelan walking up the nave of the Pro-cathedral with a silver staff in his hands. The only footage they had that was new was of young Behan, standing outside the Archbishop's Palace reading a prepared statement, saying that in time the Church would be making a comprehensive statement on the matter. Although Behan was looking suitably solemn, Christopher felt he could spot his excitement at being at the centre of a scandal that was topping the news bulletins, at getting a prime time advertisement for his professional services while also getting paid.

Afterwards his mother said that she watched the news only when he visited. 'It's always depressing. What's the point of learning about all these terrible things. God don't we have enough to be going on with?'

When she started to watch one of her soaps, full of marital disharmony and distraught teenagers, he left the room and went to the kitchen. He turned on his mobile phone and saw he had twelve missed calls. Most of the messages were from journalists, apart from one from Buzzie Hogan's solicitor, Simone, the woman he had seen in the hotel the day before, checking that Christopher would still be able to attend the meeting they had scheduled for the next day. 'We've been in London all day and it was just now that we learned about all this bother you're in. So maybe you could text me to confirm you can come.'

He texted her back confirming that he would attend the meeting. Hogan had a large plot of land just back from the seafront near

Clontarf which he wanted to develop. The city had given special planning permission allowing it to breach the height restrictions that normally applied. The city was about to get a new, high-rise, commercial quarter halfway between the city centre and the airport. There had been uproar about the granting of planning permission, but the government had rowed in behind Hogan and he was now all ready to go. The Church had agreed to sell Hogan some land that formed part of the site, and Christopher was meeting him so they could settle a few remaining difficulties. The site was important to the development since it allowed for adequate access, and Hogan had agreed a phenomenal price.

Another message was from Mary O'Mahoney, who said she had heard him on the radio and wanted to speak with him about an important matter concerning the Church.

He called her on the number she had left for him.

'Thanks for ringing me, Christopher,' she said after he had introduced himself. Again there was something knowing and inappropriate about her tone.

'I have to see you. I have something to tell you,' she said.

He said he was taking a few days' leave, but she wasn't put off so easily.

'It won't take long, Christopher. It's important.' He agreed to see her in two days' time, on Wednesday, even though he did not want to.

Heading back to the sitting room, Christopher thought of the glass of white wine he would have as soon as he got home, and felt guilty for wanting to get away from his mother so he could have a drink.

When he went back into the room, she was sitting on the sofa and laughing.

'You should watch this,' she said. 'It's a howl.'

His mother had a large colour TV and a DVD player. Christopher had neither. Bernie, the woman who tidied the house for an hour, twice a week, had come up with the idea of giving his mother loans of DVD box sets of old TV programmes that belonged to her family and which came with their recommendation. The idea had proved a great success. The latest loan was a television series about a man in the United States whose father had come to stay with him in his apartment. Christopher's mother had told him how much she liked the series, but he had never watched it. Now he sat on the sofa and watched, bored at first but not for long. The father, when he moved in, had brought with him a large TV and an old easy chair the holes in which he had fixed with tape, much in the way Christopher's father had dealt with the cracks in the ceiling of the hall. The son, a psychiatrist, had a fancy apartment filled with expensive furniture of which he was hugely proud, and was ashamed when visitors called and saw his father's old chair. The item of furniture was cleverly used to provide a focus for the tension created by the father taking up residence with the son. As the programme neared its end, both Christopher and his mother were laughing, the laughter of each infecting the reaction of the other. There were tears on both their cheeks as the final credits rolled.

'Ah god, that's a great programme,' his mother said, turning off the television with the remote control. 'I love a good laugh.'

He had forgotten how therapeutic it could be.

'You remember Mrs Ryan?'

He said he did.

'I met her at the shop last week and she told me a great joke.'

He couldn't remember his mother ever telling a joke before.

'Two athletes meet at the Olympics and one says to the other. "Are you a pole vaulter?" And the other one says: "No, I'm German. But how did you know my name was Walter?" '

She sat back in her chair and laughed freely. He joined in, mostly in response to her good cheer. He looked at her, so insubstantial and so close to death's door, and wondered if she'd ever been so happy. He felt his heart swell with admiration and with love.

He helped her out of her chair when he was leaving. Out in the hall she asked him to go so she could lock the door after him. He leaned down and kissed her cheek, opened the door and left. She closed the door behind him without further ceremony and he could hear the chain and bolt being set. He stood on the step outside the front door until she had turned off the light in the hall. The house had been too big for her for years, but it was her desire that she would finish her days there.

Walking down the hill, he remembered the joke again and smiled. He would have to remember to tell it to John. And he thought of how in all of the Gospels there wasn't one good joke.

EIGHT

THE NEXT AFTERNOON CHRISTOPHER went as arranged to the city offices of the developer Buzzie Hogan. The building was on the banks of the Liffey, in the docks. Hogan's offices were on the top floor of a premises he had built and now owned. The porter behind a desk in the ground floor lobby checked that he had an appointment, then used a swipe card when arranging for the lift to take Christopher all the way to the top floor. The lift opened onto an expansive lobby, at the far end of which was another desk from behind which a strikingly attractive young woman, wearing a simple and flattering grey dress, walked out to greet him.

'He'll be a few minutes,' she said, not mentioning Hogan by name. She was wearing lilac-coloured canvas runners. 'Can I get you something? Tea? Coffee?'

'No, thank you. I'll just have a look around if you don't mind.'

'Your first time here?'

'Yes.'

'It's cool, isn't it?'

'Yes,' he said. 'Very cool.'

There was a long coffee table with untouched copies of that day's newspapers on it. The headline on the front page of *The Irish Times* was 'New Crisis in Dublin Archdiocese', while that of the *Irish Independent* was 'Archbishop Lied About Money, Alleges New Bishop'. A picture of his face was the main photograph on the *Times*, while his and Whelan's images shared the front page of the *Independent*. John had sent him a short text that morning: 'Have you seen the papers? !!!' They had yet to talk.

Christopher chose not to sit but instead walked to the glass window that filled the wall behind the receptionist's desk. The view looked out over the roofs of the south city, towards the new rugby stadium in Ballsbridge and beyond that towards the mountains. People sometimes referred to Dublin as the city of church spires, but now the grey spires were hopelessly outnumbered by yellow cranes. The river below was full, the water lapping at the upper reaches of the quay walls. Down towards the bay he could see a large container ferry making its way towards port.

The receptionist was busy typing. Beyond her there was a corridor and offices with glass walls so that he could see that some were empty while others were occupied with people on the telephone or staring at their computers. These bankers, accountants and stockbrokers who helped Hogan manage his property portfolio and his money had themselves become millionaires over the years, Christopher knew, through their small percentage shareholdings in Hogan's various schemes. Hogan was king in this building, and these were the members of his court.

On the other side of the room, opposite the corridor, was a wall of opaque glass and a single wooden door that Christopher presumed was that of the inner sanctum.

He walked back over to the coffee table and beyond it to a large wall where paintings and framed photographs were hung randomly gratuitous. There were oil portraits and still lifes that were obviously old, some modern art, including abstract paintings with irregular edges, and black and white photographs of people and scenes Christopher did not recognise. He stood in front of a black and white photograph of a young dark-skinned woman who was naked from the waist up and was staring with great seriousness back at him, as if displaying her firm and dark-nippled breasts in a spirit of defiance. He found it hard not to focus on her breasts, to stare at them as if they might, were he to stare long enough, reveal something. But what could they reveal? Nothing, obviously. He searched the features of her face, looking for the reason for her defiance, her apparent anger. Was it because the photographer, probably a man, and now him, the viewer, wanted to stare at her breasts? Or was it because her breasts were so beautiful and so much a part of her, and her defiance had to do with her rejection of the shame others had told her she should feel? Or was it the simple, angry demand that she be loved? He looked into her dark proud eyes and felt with great acuteness the depth of his ignorance.

'Ah, the man of the hour!'

Hogan was striding into the centre of the huge room. The glass wall of his inner office was no longer opaque, the change having occurred while Christopher was staring at the photograph of the young woman.

'Jesus, you're up to your neck in it! All over the news!'

Christopher walked towards him and the two men shook hands.

'If you worked for me, you'd be fucking fired. I'd sue you and leave you with nothing, though you probably have nothing anyway. Come in! Have you been here before? This is my little nest in the air. Did Chloë not get you a tea or something?'

Hogan's personal office was even greater in floor area than the lobby outside. There were two large tables on which stood architects' models of some of his developments. There was a large table with chairs that might be used for board meetings, a low sofa and armchairs around a coffee table, and Hogan's enormous desk, on which there was little but some papers, a phone and a laptop. Again, paintings and photographs were hung in a seemingly haphazard manner on the walls. The paintings were both figurative and abstract, and Christopher noted that they included a large painting of a nude woman lying on a sofa with sunlight streaming in through a window to warm her cream skin. It was the power of nakedness that made people want to have it covered, he thought.

Simone Farrell was sitting in one of the leather armchairs, her straw-coloured hair gathered in an old-fashioned bun. Before her on the table was a cardboard folder with some pages on it, a glass and an opened bottle of water. There was nothing to indicate to Christopher that she remembered seeing him in the hotel corridor with Mary O'Mahoney stroking his head.

'Hi,' she said, not getting up, smiling kindly.

'You know Simone, don't you? Not a face any man would be likely to forget.'

Christopher said hello. He didn't respond to Hogan's comment.

The photographs on the walls recorded people and events from Hogan's life, many showing him with politicians and people from the arts world. In one he was standing beside Philip Brady as the Taoiseach cut the ribbon across the entrance to a shopping centre. Another showed Hogan standing on a large yacht in some foreign port, wearing a skipper's jacket and hat, and clutching a glass of white wine. There was one of him standing on a street in Manhattan, where he had famously bought an unused office building and redeveloped it as an exclusive hotel, which he then sold at an enormous profit.

Near his desk was a photograph of his two teenage children. Hogan had married young but had been divorced for some time. His busy and apparently very open love life was a constant in the Sunday and tabloid press. Christopher had often walked into newsagents to be confronted by front-page pictures of a smiling Hogan, standing alongside a buxom young woman whose waist he was holding, and headlines that screamed the latest development in his romantic affairs.

Two walls of the office were floor to ceiling glass windows. One looked across the river and the city towards the mountains, the other looked down the river towards the open sea. Shining new office blocks were visible in both directions, proclaiming the country's economic boom. Not an inconsiderable number of them had been built by Hogan, and some of them he still owned.

'Have you seen this?' Hogan asked.

He was standing by the glass wall that looked out onto the lobby. 'Watch.'

He gently touched the glass with a fingertip. The glass turned bottle green and opaque.

'See.'

He touched the glass again, ever so gently, and it cleared. The receptionist looked in at them and smiled, then returned to her typing.

'How fucking cool is that? I have a gadget in my desk from which I can control all the glass.'

He walked close by Christopher and tapped him on the shoulder as he passed, using the open palm of one hand. The scent of his cologne hung in the air.

'Sometimes,' he said, 'I have business in here that I don't want the others to see. Isn't that right, Simone?'

'I wouldn't know,' she said.

Hogan laughed. The sound was loud enough to fill a cathedral. There was badness in his laugh but Christopher did not dislike Hogan. He disapproved of his avarice, his womanising and the lengths he went to avoid paying his taxes, but he couldn't help but admire his zest for life and its pleasures, and even envy it somewhat. Other enormously wealthy developers he knew seemed dead inside, smothered with their secrets and their greed and their fake religiosity, but Hogan was entirely unhypocritical; he openly acknowledged the fact that he was a scoundrel. And Christopher could not but be impressed with the satisfaction he derived from his appetites.

'Come and look.' Hogan positioned himself beside an architect's model of the new commercial quarter he was going to build. 'This will be the biggest, most ambitious, most expensive development of the boom. Everything will be high spec. We've spent a fortune on architectural fees. This development will make waves around the world, act as a calling card. It will be a permanent monument to Ireland's prosperity.'

Just about every aspect of the project had been a matter of controversy. Three enormous commercial blocks, which would be visible from everywhere in Dublin, were to serve as 'iconic features' of the project, which was being called the Seafront Towers. Hogan was building on what had been football pitches and scrubland. The site was near the seafront, between the outer city and the beginning of suburbia. He had paid an astronomical amount for the land, but because the government had intervened to allow for the breaching of the city's height restrictions, the venture was now a commercial proposition. Christopher presumed that Simone, and other members of Hogan's core staff, through their minuscule percentage stakes in the scheme, each stood to reap many hundreds of thousands of euro, if not more, from the development.

As well as the signature towers, there was a park with tennis courts and a running track, a building housing a gym and a 50-metre pool, a convention centre, hotels, restaurants, cafés, underground car parks, a small central bus station connecting the development with the city centre and the airport, and a shopping centre, on the roof of which would be a helipad. It was astonishing that such a development was being envisaged for an economy that, just a decade earlier, had been considered the most dysfunctional in western Europe. Apart from some environmentalists and a number of outraged local residents, most people in the country had reacted to the project with a sense of nationalistic pride.

'We're in discussions with blue chip US multinationals. They love the short distance to the airport. We're going to have tech companies, banks, financial services, legal services, back office systems, hedge funds, you name it, all high end, top price lettings. If we can find another two outlets for them, a retail multiple that doesn't already operate here might move in, shake up that whole fucking market, bring food prices down. The Office of Public Works is looking at moving a state agency to it. A number of investors are considering pitching to have a small private clinic cum hospital in one of the towers. The fucking nay-sayers who said it was too big for such a small city, are going to be proved wrong once again. And I'm going to make millions. Fucking millions!'

Simone had come over and was standing on the other side of Hogan. The detailed architect's model included cars, a few pedestrians, a helicopter on the helipad. When she put a hand out and moved one of the model cars down a street, Christopher noticed her small watch on its simple black leather strap, her otherwise unadorned hand and wrist. He looked over at her, so strong and intelligent-looking, so poised and assured. It seemed Ireland was suddenly full of such people, fit, outgoing, university-educated, presumptive of their place in the cornucopia that was the Western World.

'Here's the Church land here,' she said.

She moved the car down the road to where the development ended in a strip of green lawn. Beyond the strip was a line of the semi-detached houses with front and back gardens which lined the road that looked out onto the sea. Hogan had at one stage planned to buy out the residents and knock down the houses, but the uproar had been such that he had dropped the plan.

The Archdiocese owned the land on which part of the entrance road to the scheme would be constructed, as well as the strip that would provide additional green space for the workers in the huge office blocks.

'It makes a key contribution to the balance of the development.'

Christopher smiled at her, wondered at the extent to which she was excited by the project, or whether she was merely professionally engaged. The development left him entirely unmoved. The boom had failed to impress him, though he had appreciated that it was a good thing that the young people of the country no longer had to emigrate, and that tens of thousands of people were getting an opportunity to lift themselves out of relative poverty through their own labours. But it had all come at a price: a fascination with economic growth; more expensive houses; the constant calculation of theoretical net financial worth. Society had become dazzled, and the Church had seemed less relevant than ever.

Simone had some documents in the vanilla folder and he and she sat down at the boardroom table to consider them. He read while she sat patiently opposite. Hogan went to the laptop on his desk and considered whatever information he was accessing there. Once or twice he fired a question at Simone. On another occasion he picked up the phone and called the receptionist, told her to confirm one meeting and cancel another. Even when quiet and focused on his work, he radiated energy.

'Everything seems to be in order,' Christopher said to Simone.

'I'm buying my place in heaven with this one,' Hogan said from behind his desk. He stood. 'I don't want any of that camel and the eye of the needle shite after this deal. I don't make a practice of being so generous. So let's keep this to ourselves.'

He let out a chuckle and came over to the low table, where he sat on the arm of Simone's chair.

'Though I am well known for giving shelter to outcast women.'

Simone was the chairwoman of a charity that ran a refuge for battered women in the city. The refuge was housed in a former fire station and the Church owned a rarely used hall on a small plot of land beside it. As part of the Seafront transaction, Hogan was going to pay the Church for the hall and to give it to the charity. The Archdiocese was more than willing to sell the property, given the use Simone's organisation wanted to make of it and the amount of money it was getting from the entire transaction. Simone had suggested that Christopher might want to join the board of her charity, but John had queried if this was a good idea given its secular and feminist ethos.

Christopher had read the documents Simone had prepared in relation to the hall's transfer. Again the price being paid was surprisingly generous.

'That all looks fine.'

Hogan said he had a series of crucial meetings with his bankers in London the next day. Simone would be travelling with him and they would be away until Friday. It was agreed that solicitors for the Church would arrange for Christopher to sign the documents on behalf of the Archdiocese in relation to both property transfers. When Simone returned from London, she would sign on Hogan's behalf. The two sides would then swap papers and the money would be transferred.

'Lots of money,' Hogan said to Christopher, a wicked smile on his face.

Christopher quoted from John's Gospel: 'Whosoever drinketh of this water, shall thirst again: but whosoever drinketh of the water that I shall give him, shall never thirst.'

Hogan laughed his huge laugh.

'You fuckers are always on the case, twenty-four seven. It's what I most like about ye. Your resemblance to me.'

Christopher addressed Simone.

'It's what Jesus said to the woman from Samaria whom he met at a well.'

'The woman seemed to like Jesus,' Hogan said.

'Well,' said Simone, 'they say power is the ultimate aphrodisiac, and you can't get much better than being the Son of God.'

The crass nature of the comment shocked Christopher and he struggled to hide how disappointed he was with her.

Earlier Simone had invited him to see the refuge and he had accepted. Now he was sorry that he had not cried off. Nevertheless he said he would wait for her outside in the lobby. Hogan walked out the door with him, stopped and shook his hand warmly.

'All that stuff in the papers and on the telly doesn't appear to be getting you down,' he said.

'It seems kind of unreal to me.'

'I know what you mean,' said Hogan. 'But believe you me, it is fucking real. I'd talk to Simone if I was you. She's saved my balls in the past. She's one in a million.'

NINE

AND SO CHRISTOPHER AND SIMONE walked into the vesperal city. He asked her about her past and she spoke willingly and openly. He stayed silent and listened. She told him she had come up to Dublin from Longford to study law in university and that during her student years she had developed an interest in women's rights and, through that involvement, had become a voluntary supporter of the refuge.

The more she told him about her activities, the more his faith in her was restored. It was a cool evening. She had swapped her light-brown leather shoes for a pair of white running shoes, and had put on a cream raincoat. The streets and pavements were busy with people going home from work.

'And when I graduated, I got a job with Hogan, because he knew an uncle of mine. I found working with him interesting, but not all that interesting. I mean, you were pursuing projects and overcoming obstacles, and there was plenty of money involved, but it's not the sort of thing you dream of doing with your life. It was strangely barren. Existentially. On the other hand, sometimes it was fun and I couldn't think of anything else to do, and I was making a very decent living. I was young and learning about the world. One day he called me into his office. At that time Hogan had a medium-sized solicitors' practice but was already spending most of his time on his investments. Not just in property. He called me into his office and said the Irish economy was beginning to grow, was catching up with the rest of western Europe, and that Irish property prices would have to catch up too. He said he was going to bet the house on this happening. Bet everything. So he did. He sold the practice, and all his shares, and put everything into property. And it worked out better than his wildest dreams. And the more the business went well for him, the more the banks wanted to give him, and the more he borrowed, the more he made, and the more he made, the more they wanted to give him, and so on. And it was all eat, drink and be merry. And he kept a lot of what he built or renovated, and became the owner of a property portfolio that just exploded in value, giving him the capacity to borrow even more. And his rent roll kept going up and up, allowing him borrow more. It all happened so quickly and it was exciting, because the numbers kept getting bigger and bigger.

'I was getting pretty rich too. Yet I felt the money was leading me by the nose, dictating the course of my life rather than giving me the freedom to live my life as I wanted to. The problem was, and is, that I don't know what else I want to do. I like having money, and a nice life, and you get a constant adrenalin rush when you work with Hogan. He's not called Buzzie for nothing. But I just know I don't want to be slaving all my life to become even richer when I already have more than I'll ever need – so much it kind of appals me.

'So one day I sat down with him and I said, "Buzzie, I want to get out. I want to do something else with my life." And he said, "Jesus, Simone, don't abandon me now, I have these two big projects coming up, and what about the one we're working on," and blah-de-blah-de-blah, and he offered me even more money. So I said I would stay for another year. But I also screwed a bit of money out of him for the refuge. That was around the time we bought the old fire station and converted it. Soon after that the board asked me to become chairwoman and I agreed. I don't really have the time for it, but when you meet the women and see the danger they're in, the needs they have, you can't look away.'

In his work as a priest Christopher had learned how to listen. But this was different. She wasn't treating him in that way.

'About two years ago I tried to leave again. This time I actually presented him with my decision. But he took me out for lunch, talked to me about his plans, including the Seafront Towers project, and begged me to stay, just to see that one off the ground. He offered me an extra percentage in it, which by the way is very hush, hush, the others don't know, and I screwed some more money out of him for the refuge, and here I am, wealthy beyond belief, and when the Seafront Towers project goes ahead, I'll be double that again. And yet I'm still Buzzie's prisoner.

'So that's me,' she said. 'Poor little rich girl. Now you've heard my confession.'

There was no sign on the refuge building to indicate what it was. The door was made of metal and the ground floor windows were bricked up. Simone pressed the intercom button, identified herself, and was buzzed in. The door opened into a glass porch, the far door of which would not open until the door behind was closed and a young woman at a reception desk on the far side of the small lobby gave them access.

They paused for a short talk with the receptionist, then went along a corridor, stopping in at a few offices where Christopher was introduced to some staff, all of them female. When they went upstairs, Simone brought him along narrow corridors, off which there were small rooms like monks' cells, or those of prisoners. Simone was explaining that sometimes, at night, drunken husbands would come to the refuge, bang on the front door and shout threats and vile abuse at their wives indoors until the police came and took them away. The fear of the women at such times, she said, had to be witnessed to be understood.

As they were passing one of the rooms, Christopher made eye contact with a woman lying on a single bed, a packet of cigarettes on her stomach. She was dressed in oversized pink pyjamas, and one of her hands, he noticed, was discoloured as if from a burn. He nodded and kept walking, but she spoke as he passed.

'Are you a priest?'

He walked back to the doorway. There were two small beds in the room. Pictures of pop stars and celebrities torn from magazines decorated the walls. There was a small chest of drawers covered with make-up and used tissue papers, pairs of running shoes and slippers on the floor. He noted a pair of small pink runners – those of a child

– and the strong smell of perfumed oils.

'This is Bishop Christopher, Martha,' Simone said.

'A bishop,' said Martha. 'Pleased to meet you, your Grace.'

She was still lying on the bed. The skin around her right eye was swollen and bruised. Simone explained that she was showing Christopher round the refuge and that the Church might help them acquire more space.

'We could do with more room, that's for sure,' said Martha. 'I have to share this room with my little girl, though she's so scared, that's probably just as well.'

The toenails of her bare feet were painted a lurid pink and there were small bits of tissue paper crammed between her toes. Christopher asked if he could sit on the other bed. Martha told him to do whatever he wanted – it was a free country. She had a wonderful lithe quality and strong, attractive features, despite the bruising around her right eye. Simone remained standing at the door.

'What happened to you?'

'My partner beat me up. He found out I'd drugs in the house, and he knocked the living daylights out of me.'

She sat up. Her fingernails were painted the same colour as her toenails. The bruising around her eye was yellow and black. Her nose was crooked but it looked as if that had happened years earlier.

'Heroin?'

'No! Do you think I'm mad? Cocaine. I wouldn't mind but he makes his living selling drugs. Eats the bleeding stuff, but it's not allowed in the house. That's one of his fucking rules. He has loads of fucking rules.'

She sat up on the bed.

'He likes me to stay at home and mind our precious daughter, be a good little wifey while he goes around screwing every young one he meets. So one night, when a few of the girls came around, we took some coke. Just a little. But then he found out, and he went ballistic, and here I am. He'll never see his fucking daughter again if I have anything to do with it.'

'What happened to your hand?'

Christopher felt bold enough to lean forward and take it in his. The skin was as smooth as plastic and curiously dry. The red, scarred tissue covered the back of her hand as far as the wrist. She had painted the fingernails on this hand the same bright pink as her toenails.

'He held me hand over the sink and poured boiling water from the kettle over it. The more I screamed, the more he smiled. When he gets angry, he becomes scary, real evil. He turns into the fucking devil.'

She had hazelnut eyes. A sense of how pain had been a constant in her life came to Christopher as a type of epiphany.

'Do you fancy her?' she asked him.

Christopher returned her hand to her lap and sat back on the bed. Simone was still standing in the doorway, her coat open so they could see her expensive cream dress. The broad smile on her face reminded Christopher that she had her own history; that there were aspects of life about which she knew so much more than him.

'Go on, tell the truth,' Martha said. 'You're gagging for her.'

'I'm a bishop,' Christopher said.

'Ah, bishop me arse. You're just another fucking man to me. You're all horny bastards. Of course you fancy her. I'd fancy her myself. Or are you gay – is that it?'

He told her he wasn't gay. She said it didn't matter to her. She hated men, she said. 'I wish I was fucking gay.'

Her mood changed with remarkable swiftness.

'I bet you live on your own.'

He said he did. She stood up. Christopher stayed sitting on the bed. Martha's soft pink pyjamas brushed against his knees as she began to fumble around with the items on the top of her dresser.

'You probably wash yourself every Sunday or something.'

Christopher didn't respond.

The smell of perfume in the room grew stronger. Martha touched his cheek lightly with her fingertips, then around his neck and along his hairline. She dipped her fingers in the scented oil again and then worked them through his hair. She was standing close to him, her chest directly in front of his face. The room was filled with the ointment's cloying odour. Christopher found it close to overwhelming, though not necessarily distasteful.

Martha replaced the oil in the small alabaster box where she kept it, closed the lid and sat back on her bed.

'Martha has more perfumes than your average pharmacy,' Simone remarked, shifting her handbag from her shoulder so it was hanging in front of her, between her legs.

'Yeah. I may be battered and bruised but at least I smell nice. Now you do too,' Martha said to Christopher.

When they were back out onto the street, it was dark and the traffic had eased. Christopher was unsure whether he wanted to go home and be alone in his house with a glass of wine, or if he would prefer to linger further in Simone's company. She was telling him more about the plans for the refuge and he found himself walking along beside her, going in the opposite direction to his home. They crossed the river and climbed the hill, went under the arched, enclosed footbridge connecting Christ Church Cathedral to its Synod Hall. They walked past St Patrick's Cathedral and on up Clanbrassil Street to where the Jews once lived and where Muslim traders now sold their wares. She came to a halt outside a Halal butcher that was still open. For most of the walk she had been talking and he had been listening.

'I live near here,' she said. 'Would you like to continue our talk over some sirloin steak?'

He agreed. When they went inside the shop, it was obvious that the crooked-toothed butcher knew and liked her.

Her home was on a quiet street of terraced redbricks and was modest given what she had told him about her work with Hogan. One-storey on the outside, it had a short hall and then a staircase that went both upwards and down.

'Do you drink wine? she asked, closing the door behind him so that he felt a soft waft of guilty air.

'More than I should.'

She opened the door to the front room and walked in, leaving him to follow her. He watched her cross the room and pull the curtains, turn on two lamps on the mantelpiece and a standard lamp that stood beside a stuffed armchair. There was a music system on a low table and she pushed the power button but didn't put on any music.

'I have a bottle of French white in the fridge. Mâcon-Villages. Is that okay?'

He told her he had a bottle of Mâcon-Lugny in his fridge at home. He sat where she told him to sit, in the stuffed armchair, mentioned an interview he had read once with a French farmer who had said wine was a way of communing with mother earth, a form of prayer.

'That sounds a bit pagan,' she said. 'I'd like to have a shower and change. I'll bring you up a glass of wine and then leave you here for a bit. Is that okay? Play some music if you want.'

She came back with a large glass of the pale, greenish-gold liquid, smiled and went away. He took a deep, greedy sip, relishing the shock of satisfaction that rushed through his nervous system. Then he stood to have a look around the room.

TEN

Later they were down in Simone's kitchen, a large room with a plain wooden dining table at the end opposite the cooker. The skillet was heating on a gas-flame while she busied herself at the sink washing spinach. Sliding glass doors looked out onto a small backyard, where weak lights illuminated shrubs and small trees that grew in large earthen pots. He had seen mention in the newspapers of Zen gardens and wondered if this was one. The table was set with cutlery, candlesticks, salt and pepper, and two glass jugs, one of water and one of silky red wine.

Her glass had been replenished and she poured what remained of the Mâcon-Villages into his glass and handed it to him. He was asked to light the candles and cut some bread, which he did, putting the bread into a beautiful blue and white china bowl she gave him. When she threw the steaks onto the skillet, they sizzled violently and the aroma of seared meat shot through the room.

'Bread, steak and salad – is that okay?'

'Wonderful.' He crossed the room and picked up the bottle from which she had decanted the red wine. It was from a château in the Loire, and looked expensive.

She slid the steaks onto two simple white plates.

'I suspect,' she said, 'and I hope, that that particular bottle is out of your price range.'

She had quartered a lemon and suggested that he squeeze some of its juice onto the steak, a new idea for him. She also recommended some raw garlic and he went along with that too. The steaks were large, his especially, and as he ate he felt how the food was providing ballast against the wine he had already drunk. The red was magnificent, banishing any doubt but that the supper was something special. After a few bites, she suggested that they slow down, and savour the food and the wine, and he did so, but with effort.

'Do you live alone?' he asked.

'Yes,' she said, after a pause, and he wondered what qualification or objection it was that she had considered before her monosyllabic answer.

'And you?'

He told her about his house in Broadstone, the street, Mrs Lacey, the nearby Basin that was the city's original reservoir, and the surrounding public park. He began to tell her about the woman who used to own the house and how she had died, but he decided that he was rambling and pulled himself up.

'This is great,' he said. 'Thank you. I'm having a really lovely time.'

She told him she was too.

'Why aren't you married?' he asked.

She laughed.

'I'm sorry. I'm not used to dining alone with an attractive woman, and drinking wine and talking. I'm not sure how I'm supposed to conduct myself. The truth is I have an enormous desire to ask you questions. I won't if you mind.'

She lifted her glass and took a sizeable sip. Her brown eyes were sparkling from the candlelight but also, he sensed, because she was pleased by what he had just said. He was surprised by how simple the transaction was; he found her attractive, and when he told her this, she in turn was pleased with him.

'Go on. If I don't like any of your questions, I'll tell you.'

'Did anyone ever ask you to marry?'

'Would you be surprised if anyone had?'

'No. On the contrary.'

'Well, thank you.' It took him a moment to realise what she meant.

'I ask because lots of people don't get married. Younger people. As if the idea doesn't apply to them any more.'

She said she had been asked once, by a man she had been going out with for some months, and whom she had really liked.

'He said he was in love with me, and he wanted us to get married and he would work and earn money and we would have a beautiful home and we would have children and I would be their mother and we would all eat together every evening. It wasn't that I didn't find that idea appealing, but . . . I like my independence, and the fact that I am successful, and at the time – it was more than ten years ago, I was in my late twenties – I felt I was too young. I wanted to see what would happen. What he was offering was too predictable. So I suggested that we wait, but he was restless, and he left me, and he's married now to someone else. They have two lovely children, but I'm not sure the wife doesn't feel a bit trapped, or that she gave up on life too easily. Or too early. And yet sometimes when I meet them and I see their beautiful children, I'm jealous, and I wonder if I might not have been better off to at least have had children with him, whatever about getting married. But he was in too much of a hurry to be middle-aged. The irony is that now I'm middle-aged anyway.'

'Do you have a boyfriend?'

'You're very interested in my personal life.'

'That's because I so rarely meet anyone who has one.'

She laughed again. He let himself think she was enjoying his company, an idea that was as intoxicating as the wine.

She said she had boyfriends from time to time, but Hogan was very demanding, and she was that little bit older. 'The men my age that are available are all weirdos. The good ones have been taken. You get offered choices when you are young and you hesitate about taking them because you don't want to lose your freedom. You don't realise that you lose your freedom anyway. Young people think choosing not to do something is a way of retaining their options, but that isn't the case. Every decision, even the decision not to decide, narrows the person's options. Time's arrow and all that.'

She smiled at him, refilled his glass, and then her own. There was no ignoring her change of tone, the increased seriousness, the wine-induced rambling.

When he asked if she was saying she regretted not having children, she said that wasn't it at all. When she was younger, she thought she could have everything, as most hopeful young people did, but she now knew that this wasn't so. 'When you spend your time doing one thing, that means you haven't spent that time doing other things. There is something inescapable about that. 'I have a beautiful house that I love. I'm rich. I've got friends whom I love. I've got so much. But it's like trying to close your hands on water, on smoke. It slips through your fingers.'

'What does?'

She looked at him for a moment, as if assessing the extent of his stupidity.

'Everything,' she said. 'Everything.'

She didn't continue and he was afraid to ask her to. For a moment he feared the evening might end in embarrassment and failure. Then she apologised for blathering and said she wasn't making herself clear.

'I'm not saying I regret having done one thing rather than the other with my time. What I'm trying to say is trite I suppose. It's that I have reached an age where it is abundantly clear how finite youth is, how quickly time passes. Sometimes I wish I'd had more fun. And at other times I wish I'd had less fun, and that I'd done more good – like you.'

He mentioned the refuge, said it was his view that the key issue was whether or not people were good in the course of their lives, as friends, parents, children, neighbours, and in their work, whether as lawyers, carpenters, shopkeepers or bishops. 'Being good cannot be an expert or a specialist role.'

She asked him if he would like some cheese and he said he would. She opened another bottle of the Loire wine.

'I shouldn't,' she said. 'I'm going to London tomorrow for some very serious meetings. You wouldn't know it from Buzzie's manner but he is under enormous pressure from his bankers. He's hugely leveraged. If people knew the figures, they'd gag. I shouldn't be telling you. Even the bankers don't know the full extent of it.'

She went to another room, returned with a board on which there was some pungent Brie and a thick slice of quince jelly. In the brief moment she had been out of the room, he'd had time to reflect on how drunk he was.

'Let's use our dinner plates. Okay?'

'Perfect.'

She cut some cheese and jelly and put it on her plate where it mingled with smears of blood from the steak. He wondered if she was lonely.

'My mother told me a joke yesterday. Would you like to hear it?'

He told her the joke. The way she laughed reassured him that the evening was going well.

'Now I'd like to quiz you,' she said. 'I've read the newspapers, the trouble you've caused because of what you said on the radio. Were you trying to cause trouble for someone?'

'Oh, let's not talk about it.'

'It's a bit late for discretion.'

'No. It's not that. It's just, you have no idea how nice it is for me to forget about the Church, meet someone like you, have a personal conversation over a lovely meal and a bottle of wine. I've never done anything like this before.'

'What? Sit down for a meal with someone?'

'It's not just that.'

She looked at him for a moment, then decided to acknowledge that she understood what he meant.

'Are you very lonely?'

'Yes. I think all priests are. We're all actors in a way. We act out our role in the community which, when you think about it, is a very particular one. Spiritual leaders, and what do we know? And then we *become* the role. And if you're lucky, you sometimes forget the loneliness.'

Her hair was dry again after her shower and her face was framed by gentle curls.

'What about sex?'

He blushed. 'I don't know anything about sex.'

She immediately started laughing and after a moment he did too. He said he had read about sex, and had heard a bit about it in the confessional, and sometimes even sermonised about it, but he knew nothing at all about it. The more he spoke, the more she laughed.

'We're always talking about relationships and the sanctity of the body and God's gift of procreation and so on, but what do we know? We all live alone in our cold, sad houses and when we're together we skirt the subject as if it was a terrifying dog that we hope won't bite us if we pretend not to know it's there. We're scared of women, especially young women and, most especially of all, beautiful women. There's something blasphemous about that, I always think. As far as I can see, Jesus was totally at ease with women; but his Church is scared silly.'

She was delighted by everything he'd said. Her face was glowing and he knew that his was too. She raised her glass and sipped, asked him if he believed priests and nuns should be allowed to marry. He said he did. He told her that the policy of priests being celibate arose in the Middle Ages, when some orders began to create enormously wealthy farming enterprises out of the forests that then covered Europe; that the abbots who ran these monasteries were the heads of great commercial operations, the equivalent of today's multinationals, and the Church didn't want them leaving monasteries to their children rather than to their order or their diocese. The problem was resolved by the introduction of celibacy. The threat of inheritance then fell way.

He knew he was going on too much, but he found it hard to stop.

'Of course, Christ said people should leave their families and follow him. But the origin of the church's policy of celibacy has its roots in property, not theology.'

'So why don't you say that?'

'It is a top-down organisation. Priests are trained to be obedient. You have no idea. To be disobedient is not simply to cross a superior; it is to go against God's will. Disobedience can imperil your immortal soul. It is not so long ago, remember, that pronouncements of the Holy Father were considered infallible. Even this – this conversation over wine with you – is exceptional in my experience. I am not used to speaking freely.

My heart is fluttering with worry. And if my Archbishop were a fly on the wall, he would be a fly with a very severe frown.'

She closed down the topic by saying she used to smoke. She said she would love a cigarette, to finish the meal. When she was younger, and it was allowed, she would dance and smoke at the same time in nightclubs, feeling the strength and wellbeing of her body, the magic of the night, the alcohol in her veins, and the nicotine.

'I don't know much about dancing either,' he said.

'Oh, I just think that's tragic. When I was younger, I used to go to pubs with my friends and afterwards we'd go to this particular nightclub where there was a wonderful DJ and I would spend hours on the dance floor. I can't tell you how much I loved it. I would dance til dawn and then walk home through the empty city exhausted and at peace.'

She stood up, said she was going to the bathroom. When she was away, he cleared the plates from the table, went back and sat down again. The candles were burning low, the room lit otherwise only by a single lamp. The silence was absolute and when she was coming back down the stairs he heard the steps creak. What will happen now? he wondered. He did not want the night to end.

'Here,' she said. 'Help.'

He stood up as instructed and helped her move the table to one side. She smiled at him and he thought maybe she had fixed her hair and put on lipstick when upstairs. She turned on the overhead lights, then dimmed them, then went to the corner where the lamp was and where there was a small music player on a low table.

'Now I'm going to proselytise.' She slipped off her shoes. 'Don't step on my toes.' She whispered the words in what he knew was a seductive tone as she moved close to him and took one of his hands. She rested her head against his chest, stood so her body was touching his. When the music started he recognised the Adagio in G minor often attributed to Albinoni. It didn't strike him as suitable music for dancing. She nestled into him and started, ever so slowly, more to sway than to dance. He put his cheek against the top of her head, all but swooned as he breathed in the perfume of her shampoo. 'Come on,' she said, 'move.' He did the best he could. His penis stiffened against her but she acted as if she did not mind. They continued to dance through a second equally slow, Baroque Adagio, barely moving, his nose buried in the warmth and scent of her hair. He relaxed and allowed himself sink into the moment.

What he felt was the heart's huge capacity for sensual love.

ELEVEN

When the music came to an end, Simone pulled back her head and looked up at Christopher. He responded as if he was doing something in which he was well practised, brought his face down to hers so their lips could meet. Her hands behind his back were willing him to continue, and after some moments he was astonished to feel her curiously stiff tongue push its way into his mouth.

'I can smell Martha's perfume,' she said when they stopped, her somehow eager eyes looking straight into his. 'Come on,' she said, and she took him by one hand and led him up the stairs out of the kitchen. He followed, thinking that this was what he really wanted, and that it was wrong. He followed her along the hall questioning whether something that felt so compelling and so right could truly be wrong. She walked ahead of him and he followed her bare feet up the stairs, watched the lovely rise of her bottom inside the blue, flower-patterned skirt she had put on after her shower, walked through the perfume she left behind her in the air.

She paused at the bathroom door, kissed him again, told him to go on. Nervously he took this as an instruction to go to her bedroom, which he did. The curtains were drawn and the green-walled room was lit by lamps on each side of her enormous bed. He sat on the bed and waited, unsure as to what it was he should do.

He thought of taking off his laced leather shoes, but he was afraid to. Could she be bringing him to her room at night, after so much wine, for any other reason than to invite him into her beautiful, warm bed? Might he take off his shoes and she return and become enraged at him for his presumption, throw him out of the house, screaming in his wake that she would let everyone know what a scoundrel and hypocrite he was? Was she bringing him to the threshold of the world of sensual pleasure, only then to forbid him entry, tell him that he understood nothing, nothing at all?

Simone came into the room and closed the door behind her. 'You look lost,' she said. When he said he didn't know what to do, she emitted a soft groan of amusement and approval that he knew he would remember to the end of his days.

'I have an early flight to London. You can stay while I get ready for bed. Is that okay?'

He said it was, though he didn't know exactly what she meant. She took a brush from the top of a chest of drawers and brushed her hair while looking in a mirror, her back turned to him. When she was finished, she used the hair itself to tie it in a bundle behind the back of her head. She ran some cream along the skin under her eyes and then came and stood a very short distance in front of him and let her skirt fall to the floor. She pulled down her underpants and left them on the floor too.

She leaned forward and kissed him, then stood back and opened some buttons at the top of her white blouse. Though the room was dimly lit, her face seemed to him to shine like the sun, her top to have a purity of white no earthly launderer could achieve. She pulled it over her shoulders and let it fall to the floor behind her. She put her hands behind her back and opened her brassiere, threw it behind her, stood there naked before him, smiling and willing him to see.

He looked. Her hair was up from around her beautiful neck and he saw how the skin folded around her bony shoulders, their unexpected squareness and strength, how her torso tapered inwards above her hipbones, the way her breasts were so rounded and fixed, so proclaiming. He marvelled at the firm muscle of her stomach, looked ever so briefly at the pubic hair below, wanted to lean forward and touch his mouth to her breasts, feel the lump of a nipple between his lips; to let himself, with what he knew would be a blessed sense of relief, lose himself in her.

She pushed him gently so he lay back onto the bed, then climbed over him like a four-legged animal. She rested herself on her elbows so that her breasts hung just below his chin, so that the most intimate part of her body was pushed against the black cotton of his bishop's shirt. She moved so their mouths could meet, kissed him long and hard, curiously desperate, he thought. He wondered that she might be pushing herself against him so as to give herself pleasure, but did not know if women did such a thing. She reached back and opened her hair so that it formed a tent to house their kissing, making for an increase in their intimacy just when he thought that might not be possible. He lay rigid on the bed, his arms by his sides, troubled with the worry that she might stop.

And then she did, without saying why. She got off him, kissed him lightly, tied back her hair, and told him to move over. When he did, she got under the covers, looked up at him and his confusion.

'This is a big deal for you,' she said.

His lack of understanding as to what she might want was, he thought, total.

'I understand completely if you want to think about it,' she said. 'Or if you don't want to go ahead with it at all.'

He moved so he was sitting at the edge of the bed and she propped herself up on one elbow so that her breasts, which had been covered by the bedclothes, became visible again. She appeared oblivious of this, though for him there was almost nothing else happening in the room.

'Do you want to kiss me goodnight?'

He was unsure about what had brought this on. Did she want him to leave? If not, then why was she mentioning his leaving?

'It's up to you,' she said, casually uttering the words he wanted least in the world to hear.

'I should go,' he heard himself say softly. Inside he screamed that he was a hypocrite, a fearful fool unable to ask for or take what it was in life he wanted.

'Kiss me first.'

He did. Afterwards he buried his nose again in her hair.

'You're so beautiful.'

'Have you ever seen a naked woman before?'

'No.'

'Do you want to look at me again before you go?'

Yes, he said, and he lifted himself off her bed as she pulled back the covers. She lay there, her arms out to each side, so he could look upon her. He let himself do what he wanted to do and he knelt down beside her bed and put the side of his face against her belly, his face towards her pubic hair, his eyes closed. He lay there for some time feeling the rise and fall of her breathing, listening to the murmurings from inside her. She placed her hands on his head and held him hard against her.

'You might as well go if you're going.'

By the time he got to the door she had covered herself again, as if ready and anxious for sleep. She said she wanted to ask him something, and that if he didn't want to answer, she would understand.

'Do you think you've committed a sin?'

He stopped himself from responding with an unconsidered no. He wanted to tell her that he was astonished by the intensity of the intimacy they had just shared, but he feared how she might respond to such a gushing comment.

'It doesn't feel wrong.'

He let himself out. Her street was empty, the night dark and full of the wonder of life lived. It was when he started to walk that he realised how powerfully excited he was. At last, he found himself thinking. At last.

TWELVE

ON THE NEXT DAY, IN THE EARLY afternoon, a taxi brought Christopher to Mary O'Mahoney's house in Foxrock. The house was on a long avenue of mature trees and old, high walls. The driver dropped Christopher outside imposing, closed gates hanging from two stone pillars, the name of the house painted on each. He examined a metal grey intercom set into one of the pillars, with numbered stainless steel buttons on it, and a grid that covered a small speaker. He pressed a large button at the base of the unit and soon heard Mary O'Mahoney's voice coming from what sounded like deep within the house. The heavy gates opened with a medieval groan.

A pebbled driveway lined on both sides by a low hedge led to the cherry red door of the enormous faux Edwardian house. The front door opened as the gates behind Christopher began to close.

'Thank you for coming,' Mary O'Mahoney said, not touching him or offering to shake his hand. She ushered him in and closed the door behind him.

The hall was so long and wide, it was more like the entrance to an institution than a home. At the end was an ornate, mahogany staircase leading towards the upper floors. An enormous chandelier was hanging some feet inside the front door but the ceiling was so high that the chandelier's lowest cut glass pearl was still a few feet above the crown of Christopher's head. There was no art on the walls, which were panelled with wood of the same dark brown as his tiny front room in Broadstone.

'Let's have something to drink, shall we, Christopher? I'm trying to get rid of as much of my husband's precious wine collection as I can.'

He followed her down the hall, under the staircase, through a door that led to the kitchen. He paused when he saw the room, astonished with a great astonishment. It was substantially greater in floor space than most people's homes. The far end of the room was constructed entirely of glass and looked out onto a manicured garden, the end or sides of which could not be seen. Along the wall to the left was a spotless kitchen area large enough to service an average restaurant. There was an island with high chairs around it, a substantial dining table with matching chairs, and a sofa opposite a coffee table and a wall-mounted, flat-screened television. On the side of the room opposite the cooker was a cocktail bar with beer taps, and wine glasses hanging upside down from shelves filled with bottles of whiskey and other spirits.

'It's a replica of Michael's favourite bar,' she said. 'He once told me he had concluded deals worth more than half a billion euro while sitting in that bar over the years.'

She walked behind the bar and took a bottle of white wine from a fridge. A large clock on the kitchen wall showed it was 2.30.

'Would you like some? Puligny-Montrachet. A Burgundy. It's Michael's house white. You wouldn't believe me if I told you how much this cost.'

He declined, thinking that with even one glass of wine, he would be tipsy again. She poured some of the wine into a glass and left the bottle standing on the bar.

She said she would make him a coffee, carried her enormous wine glass to a coffee-making machine on the far side of the room. She was wearing a loose, pink cotton top, and tight black pants. She looked fit. He sat at the island watching her while she worked. Neither of them spoke. When she was done, she put her wine, the coffee, a jug of milk, two tumblers, and a small bottle of water on a tray and suggested they sit in the conservatory. He followed her as they left the kitchen by a side door and entered a conservatory equal in size to the kitchen. Two stories high, it was host to tall ferns and fragrant, brightly coloured flowers. At the far end of a passageway there was a wicker table circled by low matching armchairs. She placed the tray on the table, sat on a chair, slipped off her sandals, and curled her legs so her feet ended on the seat beside her. Her litheness was a thing to behold.

He looked out at the expansive lawn, some old fruit trees, an area devoted to rose bushes.

'The view is magnificent in the summer, when all the roses are in bloom and the fruit is hanging from the trees.'

She showed no interest in the wine.

The coffee was delicious, aromatic and strong. He drank half of it, swallowed the glass of water she had given him, and then sipped at the coffee again. She watched him closely as he did so and he remembered what Simone had said the night before when he had told her about the appointment: 'Be careful with that woman. She's dangerous.'

Now the supposedly dangerous woman smiled at him, offered him more coffee, more water, asked him if he was tired. When she wasn't talking, the silence was complete. He presumed the house was otherwise empty. Perhaps the next house was many hundreds of metres away.

'I want to tell you a story, Christopher. Is that okay with you? Can you spare me an hour of your time?'

He was struck by how much he didn't like her. Even as he assured her that he had plenty of time, he was wondering what it was that made him feel the way he did about her. It wasn't just her false smile or her cold eyes, symptoms, he thought, of her hardness of heart. It was, he decided, an issue of perspective. He, because of his personality and the way his life had panned out, had a propensity to analyse situations in the abstract. She, he decided, interacted with the world from a perspective of relentless striving for personal advantage. He felt sure of this, even though he hardly knew the woman. He did not approve of her approach to life, but then he began to wonder if his approach to the world was not, in truth, as grounded in the search for subjective advantage (and self-protection) as hers. He dropped this line of thought as he became more interested in the story she had begun to tell.

Her husband, Michael, she told him, was the only child of a bank manager and had been brought up in a series of small towns as his father clambered his way up the ranks in bank branches around the country. Michael's father, she said, was a respectable, conservative member of whatever community he found himself living in, and, according to Michael, was incapable of expressing affection. He was a dapper, obsessively tidy man whose approach to money and to emotion were identical: 'He was neurotically mean. His wife died before him, starved all her life of affection, and he lived to be ninety-four because, Michael used to say, of his passionate desire not to be parted from his savings account and his pension.'

Her husband secured a job in his father's bank as soon as he left school and after a few years was posted to London. While there, he did the unusual thing of answering an advertisement in the *Daily Telegraph* and landed himself a job in a small English investment bank. His father, when he was told what his son had done, would have broken off relations with him there and then if there had been any relationship for him to sunder.

'The English bank had a branch in Jersey and Michael made it clear to his new employers that he would be grateful if they would in time send him there, which they did.'

She raised her wine glass, touched it to her lips but didn't drink from it, then placed it back on the low table.

'I need to tell you about Michael. He is in many ways like his father. He lusts after money, has an insatiable appetite for it. Not only that, but he has a remarkable capacity to recognise, and manipulate, people who share his interest in accumulating wealth. He is so discreet, I think he keeps secrets from himself. And, lastly, and probably most importantly of all, he hasn't an ethical bone in his body.

'In Jersey Michael got to know people who loved money as much as he did. Unlike his father, Michael was not a skinflint. He liked the good things in life, liked money not just for the feeling it gave when you had lots and lots of it, but also for what you could buy with it. 'Eat, drink and be merry' he would say. And he did. He grew to like yachts, good food and fine wine, expensive clothes, and sex. Yes. Sex. He found that having lots of money even made it easier to bed women.

'He became friendly with a rich, fast set on Jersey. He used to say that the only interest in morality they had was in the extra kick they got from knowing how bad they were being. They were older than Michael but they liked him and adopted him. They enjoyed introducing him to their vices; liked how he was always delighted, never censorious or unwilling. Some of them were bluebloods, many of them went on to receive knighthoods and become members of the House of Lords. They were the sort of people who would push old ladies off the edge of a cliff if they thought no one was looking and there was money to be made. Or even if there was no money to be made; just for the fun of it. They were debauched in a way I don't think you could ever understand, Christopher. Ever.

'What they really loved about money, in one way, was how the masses had to struggle and scrape for it, while they just sat in their enormous houses, and their wood-panelled offices, and took what belonged to others. In the end it was the combination of money and evil which excited them, made them horny even. Michael earned a lot of money. It simply fell into his lap. He screwed nearly every woman in the Channel Islands between sixteen and forty, and a few that were a good deal older. He screwed his friends' wives, sometimes with his friends' encouragement. He screwed his customers' wives and daughters. He felt he had arrived.

'Senior figures in London came to know and admire Michael. He was bright, greedy and immoral, a combination they found attractive and useful. They decided he should open an office in Dublin. Michael was to tout for business which he would then direct to the Jersey office. Ireland was having one of its temporary booms but the government was increasing its taxes on capital. Lots of wealthy people were desperate to put their wealth, especially their property, beyond the reach of the government. Michael came back here and developed a reputation as someone who was expert at helping people do just that. He began to weave a web, Christopher, with himself at the centre.'

At first Christopher had been made uneasy by the intensity with which she looked straight at him while speaking, and the way she repeatedly used his name. But as time passed he grew more relaxed. He watched her and thought how articulate and bright she was. He suspected that when she had been younger, she had been confident of how alluring she was to men, but that now she was less sure.

'As well as banking and property, he developed his understanding of company law, contract law, trust law, and so on, transforming himself into someone who could give advice on property investment, finance, company structures – the whole thing. He began to create a hidden world of offshore companies and Channel Island trusts, banking relationships and tax schemes, dirty deals and secrets. Despite what he was up to, people trusted him. He wheedled his way into the private lives of the rich and powerful, whispering in their ears, encouraging them, Christopher, to commit crimes; putting deals together, telling people to leave the details to him, that he would take care of everything, and that they would never be caught. He became an intimate of the richest and most powerful men in the land, of everyone who combined wealth with moral ambivalence, which is just about everyone who is wealthy.

'Michael found you, not the other way round. How he managed it I don't think I will ever know. He helped people shift their property and money offshore, and Michael, and his friends in London and Jersey, took a slice from everything that moved.

'Now I want to tell you a bit about myself, Christopher. I was born in Finglas. I had three brothers and two sisters and we lived in a small, terraced, three-bedroomed house. My father was a bus conductor; he was a bit rough but his heart was in the right place. My mother did her best to feed us and keep us clean. I went to school but I wasn't interested. You could feel the way the nuns, culchies most of them, looked down on us, struggled with their desire not to be in the same room as us. I left at sixteen and did a secretarial course. I got my first and only ever job in Michael's offices on Fitzwilliam Square after I answered an advertisement posted on a noticeboard in the secretarial school. He interviewed me himself. I spent hours getting myself ready, locked in the bathroom of our crowded little house in Finglas. When I went into his office and met him for the first time, I could see the look in his eyes. I knew straightaway it wasn't just my typing skills he was interested in. He's more than twenty years' older than me, but the first time I saw him, Christopher, it was like we could see into each other's souls. Three and a half years later we were married. We celebrated my twenty-first birthday on St Lucia in the Caribbean. At the time most people in Dublin had never heard of the island.'

She had not wanted to have children and neither did he. He wanted someone to keep him company, to provide a base from which he could venture forth into the world. He didn't want to change or to slow down, but he did want someone to share his success with, so that he wouldn't have to be troubled by loneliness. What she wanted, she said, was money. She loved being mistress of a large house, having others clean up after her, maintain the garden, cook meals. She liked being the wife of a rich and powerful man, liked the way other women looked at her with venom in their eyes, because of her background, the age difference between her and Michael, the obvious nature of the contract they had made.

'He still screwed everything he could. I didn't mind so much. I got used to it. I stopped going to the office, so I didn't have to see the staff and wonder which one of them was opening her legs for him. And over time, I imagined, he lost his vigour, got more interested in money and business, and less interested in jumping into bed with every greedy little bitch who was hoping he might throw a diamond necklace at her, or take her on a shopping trip to New York. I even thought, Christopher, that he might come to think it undignified for a man past retirement age to be stripping off in hotel rooms with girls just out of school. I somehow forgot about the old creeps from Jersey who made passes at me just after I married Michael. Women keep thinking they understand men, but they never do. Wishful thinking keeps getting in the way.'

Some months before she had noticed a change in the atmosphere between them, an even greater emotional distance than usual on his part. She had hired a private detective, a woman. A week later the woman had come to see Mary, carrying an envelope in which she had a few photographs, some pages from bank statements, a document from the registry of deeds.

Michael had a mistress, many years younger than Mary. That was nothing new. But what was new was that she was going to have his baby and he was still with her. He had set her up in a large apartment in the south city. Some months earlier he had transferred ownership of the apartment to her. Michael was going to set up a second home, and the child was something Mary feared she could not compete against. Everything she had given her life to was under threat.

One of the pictures the detective brought with her showed Michael with his mistress, one arm around her waist as they walked along some street Mary did not recognise. 'She was wearing a short yellow dress, and you could see the bump in her belly. Blonde, her oversized tits sticking up out of her décolletage – a real floozy. I tore the picture in two and decided to go to war.'

THIRTEEN

MARY O'MAHONEY ENGAGED A solicitor, who contacted her husband when he was away on business in London. The solicitor told O'Mahoney that his wife was instituting divorce proceedings on the grounds of adultery. O'Mahoney was told that his wife would be remaining in the family home until alternative accommodation was agreed as part of a negotiated or court-appointed settlement. The solicitor had said the whole matter could be dealt with on a confidential basis as long as O'Mahoney acted reasonably.

'That of course was code for you'd better be careful or I'll tell everything I know to the press, or even the police. My solicitor, by the way, Christopher, cost a fortune. Michael has to pay my fees as part of the final settlement. I encouraged my solicitor to charge a scandalous hourly rate.'

She was not in fact going ahead with a divorce. That suited her and it also suited Michael, who did not want people asking questions. A separation agreement had been negotiated. A large amount of money had been transferred to her bank account, and she was now independently wealthy. Michael and his 'little bitch' were to move into the house in Foxrock, and Mary was to move to a house in Killiney that had been bought for her just a week before, at auction.

'He had to pay for the house as part of the settlement, so I organised it that a friend of mine, recently divorced, pretended she was bidding for the house. She engaged a solicitor, who attended the auction while she stayed in contact on the phone. We were the last two bidders and we bid back and forth, back and forth, until we had bid up the price by an extra million. You may have read about it. It was on the front page of the property supplement in *The Irish Times*.'

She still hadn't drunk any of her wine. Christopher had finished his coffee and the bottle of water. He sat there wondering when she would start explaining what all this had to do with him. It appeared obvious that she was not about to ask him for spiritual advice. She sat up, slipped her feet back into her sandals, and stood. So much about her was perfect: her poise, her fingernails and toenails, her hair. Her body was the product not just of money but also of determination and effort. When she spoke, she looked straight at Christopher with a disarming openness. He had begun to wonder whether he did not, at some level, admire her.

'Have you ever been in a house like this before, Christopher?'

'What do you mean?'

'The house of someone who is disgustingly rich.'

He had an acquaintance who was a partner in one of the city's top accountancy firms, but his wealth, Christopher was sure, was nothing compared with O'Mahoney's.

'No,' he said. 'I suppose not.'

She offered to show him around and he accepted. He was curious but he was also conscious of a rumbling in his empty stomach, a certain light-headedness. He asked if he could have a slice of bread, or a sandwich, and she said that would be no difficulty at all. She took out her phone, dialled, introduced herself to someone with whom she was obviously acquainted.

'What's your special today?' she asked, and then, turning to Christopher, said: 'How about pan-fried sole served with olive oil and lemon juice, and a side order of spinach? Or some lasagne? They do a very good lasagne.'

He asked for the latter. She spoke again on the phone and then told him that the food would be delivered in about ten minutes. 'We can look around a bit downstairs in the meantime.'

He followed her through the house. The sitting room was huge, with two bay windows looking out on the front garden, an enormous fireplace, a number of stuffed sofas and armchairs, lots of antique furniture; gold-framed oil paintings on the walls. She went to a low table near one of the sofas and picked up a remote control.

'Watch,' she said, pointing the instrument at what he thought was an antique bureau. The slatted front of the bureau began to roll up, revealing a flat-screened television.

'There's a small private cinema in a room off the kitchen. We never watch TV or sit in the cinema.'

The front of the bureau began to close again. She picked up another remote, pointed it towards the mantelpiece, and on came the familiar voice of a presenter on the main national radio channel. He could not see where the speakers were. She said there was also a music system that operated throughout the house. The system could be played in any one or any combination of rooms. 'Not that I know how to use it. When we have parties, there is a man who organises the music for us,' she said. It was the first time in the afternoon that Christopher had noticed her using the present tense.

She showed him the dining room, which was dominated by a large stag's head that hung over a heavy mahogany fireplace. The paintings on the walls were of rural scenes, fields in sunshine, landscapes untouched by the contemporary world. On the other side of the hall was an imposing set of double doors that led into a substantial ballroom with a small stage at one end. The floor was empty apart from the cushioned wooden chairs that lined the room on two sides, and a mirror ball that hung from the centre of the ceiling.

They walked the length of the ballroom and went through a door at one side of the stage into a small hallway. She opened a door on her right and led him into another substantial room. A large window looked out onto the garden, where he could see a tennis court enclosed in high, green netting, and what he thought must be a small toilet and shower room. In the middle of the room was a billiard table, the coloured balls scattered around the green cloth, and a single cue ball lying in their midst.

'I must remember to tear that cloth before I leave,' she said.

He followed her back to the kitchen. 'Of course there are toilets everywhere, Christopher. Just tell me if you need one.'

The wine bottle was still standing where she had left it. She walked across the room, pulled back a sliding door in the glass wall and stepped out into the garden. He stood beside her, listening to the somehow incongruous singing of birds, looking out at the grass and the leaves against the blue and white of the cloudy sky. The Dublin mountains could be glimpsed through the trees.

'I'm not going to show you around the garden. There's about two acres of it and it's worth an absolute fortune. See that over there?'

She pointed at a narrow pond, its straight sides and ends marked by a small iron railing. At the end farthest from the house there was a small water feature, with water flowing down over the face and body of a bronze mermaid and into the narrow parallelogram that was the pond.

'Now come see this, Christopher.'

Back in the kitchen she opened a door in the wall and they went down a wide spiral staircase into a basement. She showed him a room off the corridor to their right. It was a dimly-lit *cave*, the bottles of wine held in floor to ceiling metal shelving arranged so that you could walk amongst the shelves and choose the wine of your fancy. She thought they might just look from the door but he went in to examine the wine labels and to think about the warm landscapes from which the wines had come.

'There are bottles in here worth tens of thousands. But I can't tell them from the ones that are only worth hundreds, or that you might get off the top shelf in Tescos.'

She suggested that he select something to go with his lasagne and when he tried to resist she insisted. He found the shelves containing Italian wines and selected a Chianti Classico Riserva because of the attractiveness of its label and the way it had a light covering of dust.

'Michael says he loves fine wine, but I suspect he doesn't know his arse from his elbow. He doesn't enjoy a wine unless he knows how much it cost.'

Christopher followed her out and on down the corridor. At the end was a large room lit with soft green and white light, most of the floor space of which was taken up by a shimmering swimming pool.

In a recess in one of the walls there were showers, and alongside them was a wooden wall and a window looking into what Christopher presumed was a sauna. In the middle of the ceiling was a long strip of daylight, and he realised they were underneath the garden pond. The daylight through the pond created a weak, green and silver shimmer on the pool's still surface. He felt he was in a magical cave, and for a moment thought of how wonderful it would be to live in a house that had such a room.

'It's a twenty-five-metre pool. Michael actually uses this room, swims about fifty lengths most mornings, then sits for a time in the sauna. I think it's the closest he comes to having a spiritual life.'

There was a rough, electronic sound and she went to a phone that was attached to the wall and buzzed someone through the gates. They went back up the spiral staircase and she left him in the kitchen and went to answer the front door. While she was out of the room, he opened the Chianti, using a corkscrew he found in the replica bar. He poured a hint of the rubicund liquid into a large wineglass, swirled it round, sniffed it, closed his eyes with pleasure, and poured himself a generous measure. It was not such a great idea but he told himself he would have only the one.

The lasagne came with a green salad and garlic bread. She laid the meal out on a white plate, got cutlery and a linen napkin, and set a place for him on the island. He ate the food and drank the wine while she sipped a glass of bottled water. When he had finished, she removed the dishes and made him another cup of strong coffee.

While this was happening she told him that O'Mahoney had a study upstairs where he kept a lot of his papers. It was his private room and he locked the door when he wasn't using it. After she had instituted divorce proceedings, she had engaged some builders who had taken the door off its frame. She had then rummaged around his office, including in his computer. Her private detective had hired an expert for her who had circumvented Michael's password in about five minutes. She had spent hours in the office, going through his files, trying to learn as much as she could. 'Most of it didn't mean much to me. However, I did find a few files that contained papers that seemed to involve dealings with the Church. And when I happened to hear you on the radio, Christopher, I thought maybe I should give you a call.'

She left the kitchen and came back with a compact disc case which she placed on the island between them. Someone had written 'Church' on it with a large black marker. Looking at the writing, Christopher realised he had not seen one book since entering the house.

'As part of my separation agreement, I have sworn an affidavit saying I have not disclosed any information about Michael's personal or business affairs to anyone. And I haven't. They also made me give a commitment that I won't do so in future. The reason I invited you here, Michael, is to breach that commitment. Breaching the commitment can allow him to sue me for everything I get from him, but of course he would have to prove it first, and he would be taking a great risk if he hauled me into court. I want to give you some of the information I've found, and I want a commitment from you that you won't tell anyone where you got it. I want you to swear not to.'

She said she wanted him to wait before answering, and invited him to continue the tour of the house. They went upstairs, saw the separate en suite bedrooms she and her husband had slept in, their two walk-in wardrobes, each of them larger in size that the largest room in Christopher's home. They walked past the locked door to O'Mahoney's study, which had been replaced so that there was no sign that it had ever been removed. She showed him some of the guest bedrooms and brought him up to the attic where a gym was arranged so that all the machinery faced a plate glass window and the Dublin mountains.

'When Michael was in the pool I would come up here, run on that treadmill, cycle on that machine there, do ten million sit-ups to keep my stomach flat. It would give me great pleasure to see him go to jail.'

He said he couldn't swear not to speak to anyone about the material on the CD. She would just have to trust him to be fair to her and to do what he thought was right. He said he wasn't sure if he should take the material from her at all, given the way she had come into possession of it, and that if he did take it, he might choose not to do anything with it. She said she thought he had a duty to the Church to look at it, that from what she had seen, it was clear there was a lot of money involved. It was only when he had examined the material and worked out what it all meant, she said, that he would be in a position to make an informed decision. She used a soft, seductive tone when urging him to take the disc, and said his name so often at the end of her sentences that he began to find it disturbing. In the end, he told himself later, it was his desire to get away from her that caused him to agree.

She phoned a taxi for him and walked with him to the gate, gave him a bag containing the two opened bottles of wine, with ornate-handled cork stoppers pushed into them to stop the wine from spilling.

'The stoppers are Victorian,' she said. 'The handles are solid silver.'

FOURTEEN

The taxi dropped Christopher outside his primrose door. 'There you go, your Grace,' said the driver, who was old and who had, in the course of the journey, made it clear that he was a pious and loyal servant of the Church. He refused to take a fare. As Christopher put his key in the door, he heard Mrs Lacey opening hers. 'Ah, the bishop,' she said. 'I hope that wine's not meant for the altar.'

He told her he had just come from the house of a rich woman who had given him the wine as he was leaving. He said he did not know the price of the wine but believed that each bottle might be worth up to a hundred euro, and possibly much more.

'That doesn't impress me if you think it does,' she said. 'You know I'm no holy Joe but I sometimes wish that there was a hell so that bitches like the woman you're talking about could be sent there. Bottles of wine for hundreds of euro. Sucking up to priests. Makes me sick. I suppose those stoppers you have shoved in the bottles are made of silver.'

He slipped one from a bottle and gave it to her, feeling the heft of it as he did so.

'Solid silver, I'm told.'

'That sort of shite just annoys me,' she said. 'When you think of the way most people have to scrape and struggle to get by, and the big shots can't check the time without having a watch that costs more than everyone else's. But I don't care really. I'm grand with what I have, and don't I have a handsome man as a neighbour? Come here. Do you want to come in for a minute?'

He said he would. A widow in her seventies who lived alone,

Christopher knew she enjoyed company. She brought him in, along a short corridor with squeaking floorboards into the room beyond. The wall between the front and back rooms had been knocked down and there was just a counter between the resulting large room and the kitchen extension built out into the yard. The television was on and, as always, blaring. She picked up the remote and turned down the volume.

'Sit down, sit down. Have a biscuit.'

He sat on one of her worn armchairs and took a biscuit, fielded her question when she asked him to identify the rich woman, agreed with her that he met all sorts in his line of work. He told her that he didn't meet that many who had as interesting a past as she had. When she protested, he insisted that having a grandmother who had been born in Bombay to an Irish soldier enlisted in the British army, and being raised on Gardiner Street with a granny who cooked the occasional curry, and could tell her grandchildren about elephants and India, was a story he had not come across before.

She said her life had been as good as anyone's and better than most. Then she asked him if he had heard what had happened to old Mr and Mrs Martin up the road. The couple were unusual on the street, in that they were both alive. Most of the older residents on the street were widows who lived alone, their husbands having died years earlier.

'This is a good one,' she said, offering him another biscuit. She stood by the kitchen counter while he sat in the armchair. 'Didn't they get an idea that they should have a holiday somewhere foreign. Get a bit of sunshine on their old skins; see if they could get some relief from their various ailments. So Mrs Martin read a few holiday brochures and decided on Tenerife. She sent your man off into town to buy the tickets, and off he went and came home with them, and they packed their bags weeks in advance and then the day came and they were off, real pleased with themselves, having made sure everyone in the place knew where they were going.

'Well they came back last week and she was all, lah-di-dah, what a nice time they'd had, and the blue sky and the blazing sun, oh and the food was only delightful. But he was down the pub and he told the lads, and now everyone knows. Didn't he buy the wrong tickets! It was only when they landed and were going through customs that they realised they'd gone to the wrong place. They were in Israel. In Tel Aviv, not Tenerife! Everywhere they went there were soldiers carrying machine guns. She spent most of her time locked up in her hotel room, afraid she might get blown up by a suicide bomber! Oh Jesus, it's gas! She'll kill him when she finds out he's let the cat out of the bag. She'll skin him alive!'

There were tears of happiness in her eyes as she told the story. He stood up when she was finished and said he would have to go. She offered him another biscuit and he said he would take it with him. After he closed his own front door, he heard through the wall the sound of her closing hers.

He put away the wine and took off his shoes, then went upstairs to the front room with his laptop and the disc Mary O'Mahoney had given him. He sat at a small table and booted up the computer. The disc contained a large amount of folders. Each folder he checked had a number of documents in it. He clicked randomly though the documents, stopped here and there to read something closely, fetched a notebook and jotted down some names. It was exactly the type of material he loved to work with. He examined property deeds, ledger entries recording payments and receipts, company filings showing share transfers, mortgages, and changes of registered address. The properties, he noted, were all Irish, most, though not all, in Dublin. The companies tended to be Irish or Jersey-registered, though a few were English. Some of the ledgers were in Irish pounds, others in sterling, while some did not disclose the currency.

Christopher connected with the internet and logged onto a service that allowed him access to the Irish and British company registries. He soon realised there was too much going on for him to follow it easily on screen and that he would have to print the documents, make his own files. A few of the names seemed familiar to him from his work for the Church. He didn't know what it was he was looking for, but experience told him that the close examination of such documents, more often than not, revealed their secrets.

He was on his way to the kitchen to take O'Mahoney's white wine from the fridge and pour himself a glass when the phone in the hall rang. It was John, offering news from Archbishop's House and the latest on the Finnegan fiasco.

'Do you want me fill you in?' he offered. 'It's been a crazy day.'

Christopher suggested he would call over to John's house and his friend agreed. He put the wine into an iced wine holder, and then into a cotton supermarket bag. He walked to Dorset Street and hailed a taxi. When he arrived at John's house, his friend was wearing tracksuit bottoms and a large t-shirt and had obviously just come from the shower. He invited Christopher to sit in his front room with him, where he had laid the table with glasses, a jug of water, bowls of olives and sunflower seeds, and a plate of oiled bread.

'I wish you would taste this wine,' said Christopher. 'It's special.'

'So is this bread,' said his friend. 'Made with real yeast.'

They had met and become friends many years earlier, when they were both, for different reasons, staying in the Irish College in Rome. They had played table tennis in the evenings and had eaten together in restaurants, discussing over their meals their dreams for the future. It was John who had introduced Christopher to the pleasure of having wine with his food. Later, however, John had forsworn alcohol, and become something of an obsessive about his health.

Christopher told John that he had been to O'Mahoney's house and of how Mary O'Mahoney had given him two bottles of wine with silver stoppers in them when he was leaving. The house, he said, was enormous, a big, empty, ridiculous thing.

'He's an able and very well connected man,' John said. 'I wouldn't trust him with my communion money, but there have been times when we've been glad to have him on our side.'

The front and back rooms of John's house, which he had moved into soon after he had been made a bishop, were connected by double doors. Both rooms were sitting rooms that also functioned as studies, and were filled with church papers, books on theology and health, and, most of all, education. After his appointment, John had become the Irish episcopate's expert on the issue of its role in the provision of education, advising the Church on how it could withdraw from a sector it no longer had the manpower to run, while still maximising the influence of the Church and its doctrine on those children who attended Irish schools. It was his passion – a focus for the energy and positivity with which he faced his days.

Christopher told John what Mary O'Mahoney had said to him about her intention to get divorced, and her eventual separation agreement, and the house that had just been bought for her. He continued his monologue knowing that among his reasons for giving John all this unnecessary information was his desire to avoid mentioning what had happened between himself and Simone. He told his friend the whole story of his visit to the lavish house in Foxrock, but made no mention of the documents he had been given. John did not notice that his story had no focus.

When Christopher had finished, he poured himself another glass of the wine and then settled back to hear John's account of the latest from Archbishop's House. He felt not the slightest twinge of guilt about his reticence concerning Simone. Now, he felt certain, was not the time.

'Whelan', said John, 'is being crucified. Hung out to dry. The Nuncio is full square behind Reilly and is positively relishing the position Whelan finds himself in. As far as the Nuncio is concerned, the more Whelan has to sweat and squirm, the better. They see it as his fault that you were made a bishop, and therefore his fault that the Church has been embarrassed. So the problem is not Reilly's mendacious report, but Whelan's judgment. Even his loyalty to the Church.'

The Archbishop was to go on radio the following morning. He was to give a live interview on Nolan's show in which he would deal with the whole affair, including his response to what the Church had known about Finnegan. 'There's not a snowball's chance in hell that he will point the finger at the Nuncio, or at the Holy Father, so he will just have to suffer public humiliation, eat humble pie, and keep mum while his good name is being dragged though the mud.'

John paused in his delivery, popped an olive into his mouth, sucked the flesh from the stone, dropped the stone back out onto the palm of his right hand, and then placed it on a plate alongside some others. Christopher had often thought that his friend would have made an excellent executive in a large company, because of his interest in, and skill at, the politics of human organisation. What made him more suited to the Church, Christopher also knew, was his profound commitment to the struggle to do good.

John swallowed another tumbler of water.

'As for you,' he said, sitting back in his armchair. 'You are beyond the Pale. You have been guilty of gross disloyalty and are now considered to be an outright enemy of the Church. Your elevation to the position of bishop is considered to have been an enormous error, one for which the Holy Father accepts no blame whatsoever, relying as he did on Whelan, and, it has to be said, on me, who recommended you and gave assurances as to your suitability to Whelan and the Nuncio. You, I told them, could be trusted.

'For that I will now have to suffer a little, though I'm embedded in so much stuff here in the Archdiocese, I don't think they will go to the trouble of moving me or upending my life in any serious way. You, however, are in seriously bad odour. The debate hasn't moved on yet to what should happen to you, but something will, of that you can be sure. Your future will be a topic of discussion in the corridors of Maynooth during the upcoming Synod. You, dear boy, are going to suffer.'

He sat forward, tossed another olive in his mouth, spat out the stone and poured himself another tumbler of water.

'If I was you, my friend, I'd start getting ready for an inhospitable clime.'

His tone was one of friendly delight.

FIFTEEN

Later, at home, Christopher found that his soul was exceedingly troubled. It had been his practice to avoid confrontation. The path of his life was the product of his desire not to be involved. Yet here he was, a cause of tension between the Archdiocese and Rome; a person whose first visit as a bishop to a Synod in the University of Maynooth would occur against the backdrop of a scandal in which he was a central character. Instead of being welcomed into the fold and being given the time and space to get used to his new position, he was to be the subject of gossip, of whispered conjecture as to what was motivating him to drag into disrepute the Archbishop who had so recently opted to place such trust in him.

Christopher was also uneasy because of what had happened with Simone. It was not so much guilt over what they had done together as it was shame that he had done something of which he in theory disapproved, and which, for that reason, he wanted to keep hidden from his friend and his church colleagues. The encounter with Simone was for him a source of inner joy and satisfaction, a thing of beauty to which he let his thoughts repeatedly return. And yet, strangely, because he was acting as if it was something about which he should feel ashamed, the memory of what they had shared was becoming shadowed by bad conscience.

And as if that was not bad enough, now he was in possession of confidential documents that apparently contained secrets that would further trouble the Church.

He went to the kitchen and fetched himself a glass, poured some of the Chianti, and went and sat on a chair in the backyard. He thought of John and the other men in the episcopate he had come to know over the years, and imagined how they would react when his time came. The Archbishop of Armagh would be severe. He would view Christopher as a trouble-maker, a reckless and disloyal person who had to be stopped from causing any further damage to the efforts of the Church to fulfil God's work on earth. It was a strange and troubling idea, to think you might be acting so as to frustrate the institution that had as its focus the furtherance of the work of the Son of Man. And that you were doing so because you were telling the truth.

John, and other bishops with whom Christopher was on good terms, would not side with him against the Archbishops, or the Nuncio. Despite what they thought of the issue, they would stay mute as their more conservative episcopal colleagues focused on the question of an appropriate punishment for Christopher. He would have to suffer having Reilly sit in judgment of his actions, and even be party to the decision as to the punishment to which he should be subjected. Banishment of some sort, no doubt, would be the favoured outcome. Time would be allowed pass, then the announcement would be made, and Christopher would be assigned to some duty far from home, away from his mother, away from the life he had constructed so as to be protected from life. Away, he found himself thinking, from Simone.

He remembered again the extraordinary experience in her bedroom. It was astonishing that such an epiphany could be so rooted in the physical. Everything about it had to do with the body. It had been a flooding of the senses that had resulted in a swooning of the soul and was, in its way, contrary to everything the Church stood for, from the teachings of St Augustine on. Yet it had felt so right, so like an arrival; a reward for all the striving that had gone before.

And yet. What had happened was not new for Simone. To experience God's love was to have an encounter with the absolute. Absolute understanding, permanent love. His encounter with Simone could hardly be more different from hers. Despite the intensity of what had happened between them, they remained strangers to each other. The next time he met her, she might make it plain that she did not like him, or tell him that she had fallen for another. She had presumably been through such episodes before. Perhaps a number of times. What had occurred between them was embedded in the temporal and was entirely subjective.

And yet. And yet.

He noted how his soul was troubled more as a result of his encounter with Simone than because of his difficulties with the Church. He stood under the star-filled sky in his small yard in the middle of the sleeping city and considered how what he desired most was that he was beside her in her London bed. His mind filled with the images of her that had been haunting him since the night before. He recalled the wonderful warmth of her scalp. The depth of his feeling as she had danced with him. Everything about what had happened seemed so good. He had not known that surrender to the senses could achieve such artistic perfection; that the trust with which a dancer's head was placed against a partner's chest could express such tenderness; that intimacy could match music, take the human beyond language and reason with such deftness and evident truth.

He saw again that moment when she had stood before him in her bedroom and taken off her clothes. To think that God's grace could manifest itself in physical form, that it could choose the body as its language, be made flesh by way of flesh itself, so that the chosen one could feast his eyes upon it and marvel.

Christopher stepped back into the kitchen and poured another glass of the expensive Italian wine, downing it in one gulp. A thought had occurred to him that had set his heart racing. Back in the yard he paced the small space like a caged beast. It was as if the sky itself was too low to accommodate the strength of his emotion. On one level his life was falling apart, yet how glad he was of what was happening. How glad. He sat on the chair again and leaned back his head to look up at the heavens. Good lord, he thought, almost laughing. Good lord.

He poured the last of the wine into his glass and took it with him to the front room. He turned on a lamp, pulled the curtains, and lay on the sofa. How beautiful it could be to be alive. Even meaninglessness could add to the tragic magnificence of where men and women found themselves, temporarily alive under the uncaring stars, inclined towards creativity, conjecture and love.

He felt a swelling in his heart and a determination that he would not be afraid.

SIXTEEN

WHEN CHRISTOPHER TRIED TO STAND, he found he was more drunk than he had thought. He stood up straight and waited until he was sure of his ability to remain upright, before putting a hand forward and switching off the lamp on the mantle of the small, tin fireplace. The room was now in darkness and he fumbled his way to the window, touched his hands against the soft material of the heavy curtains, and pulled them open to let in the light from the street.

When he did so, he found himself looking straight at the face of a young man who was staring back at him. The man had long blond hair, pronounced cheekbones and a strong jaw. He had pale eyes and was looking at Christopher, for some reason, with an expression of sorrow and understanding. A thin hand was holding on to the collar of a grey, unbuttoned linen jacket that he was keeping wrapped tightly around his neck while his other hand, Christopher imagined, was holding his penis as he pissed against the wall. Despite the suddenness of the encounter, both men remained still and calm. Then the young man, while continuing to stare intently at Christopher, lifted his hand so his linen jacket fell from his shoulders. His upper body was naked, his chest, shoulders, and stomach all lean and firmly muscled. The young man held his hands out directly from his body, not by way of imitation of the crucifixion but rather as an indication that his penis was on display. Christopher felt no inclination to look down. The nearby streetlight created a chiaroscuro worthy of Caravaggio. There was no denying the aesthetic aspects of the scene, of how the light and shadow were playing on the young man's muscled physique, his oddly plaintive but understanding expression. Nothing moved for a few seconds but then, without any reason that Christopher could ascertain, the stranger smiled and turned away.

Christopher hurried to the hall, unlocked and pulled open the front door and stepped out. There was no sign of the young man, or of the jacket that had slipped from his shoulders. He was alone on the street. All the houses were dark save Mrs Lacey's, where her silenced television was casting a blue glow through her drawn curtains. Something about the quality of the night intensified his sense of being alone. Under the same dark sky, in London, Simone was in a hotel room, her beautiful body between white sheets, her sleeping face on a soft pillow. His life had been filled with service, with the giving of spiritual succour, reading passages from the scriptures to the faithful and hearing their confessions of sin. But what did he know of the human heart? Nothing. He was hopelessly ill-equipped for being in the world, amongst others, in pursuit of love. And yet, it was clear to him now, standing alone outside the open door of his empty home, that the purpose of life was the life of the heart.

SEVENTEEN

IN THE MORNING CHRISTOPHER WOKE to find his thickened, unhappy blood thumping against his cranium. His tongue felt swollen and was sticking to the roof of his parched mouth. He made his way gingerly downstairs, clutching the handrail. After washing his face in cold water, he sat on the edge of the bath and recalled the night before, the wine, the young man at the window, and most of all the revelation that had come to him when he had been out in the yard. He found he had not changed his mind and he wanted to call Simone and tell her what had happened, but feared how she might respond. His hands shook as he took his mobile phone from the pocket of his trousers, turned it on, and composed a text message to her, telling her how he had been thinking of her and how he wanted to wish her well. After a moment's pause he sent it, and within an uncannily short space of time he received her reply.

'Hi. I've been thinking of you also. Very busy here. Will be home tomorrow evening arriving at 6pm on the Aer Lingus flight. Could you meet me? Did you have an interesting meeting with O'Mahoney's wife? Be careful. XXX. S.'

The message both delighted him and caused him concern. Still sitting on the side of the bath, he read it twice, noting the request that he meet her at the airport and the three 'x's, but also the reference to his meeting with Mary O'Mahoney. He was still pondering the message when his phone sounded, startling him with its shrill ring in the small bathroom. He was very surprised when he found himself listening to Mary O'Mahoney. She began speaking without using his name. Her tone was businesslike and curt.

'I've been ringing you all morning.'

'My phone was turned off.'

'I'm ringing you about that information I gave you. Have you shown it to anyone?'

'No,' he said, having difficulty keeping up with the pace of events.

'Have you mentioned it to anyone?'

'No.'

'Michael knows I met you, that you came to the house. Buzzie Hogan told him. What are you up to? Why on earth did you tell Hogan?'

Simone, he thought, must have told Hogan, but why would Hogan be interested?

'I haven't seen or spoken to Hogan since our meeting,' he told her.

'Well, someone told him or one of his gang, and it wasn't me, so it must have been you.'

He let the sentence hang. He could feel the truth of Simone's warning in Martha's tone. He felt a sting of betrayal arising from Simone having told Hogan, but wasn't sure why he should. He also felt a determination not to involve her.

'I had no reason to mention it to Hogan. What's it got to do with him?'

'Michael asked if I had told you anything, given you any information. I told him I hadn't but he doesn't believe me. I've changed my mind. I want the disc back. Have you looked at it?'

'Not really. What I looked at meant nothing. I've haven't had time to study it.'

He didn't know what all this was about, if anything, but it was causing a tightness in his chest and he found himself strongly resenting the stress this woman was causing him.

'Are you at home?' she asked.

'Yes.'

'I'm in town. Where do you live?'

He told her, gave her directions and hung up. He wished dearly he had never taken anything from her, and that he had never visited her in the first place. What was she doing, dragging him into her awful life? As if he didn't have enough on his plate already.

He felt wretched and knew the best thing would be tea and toast, followed by pain killers and a short walk. Despite these feelings, he climbed the stairs, booted up his laptop. He fetched the disc she had given him and put it into the disc drive to make a copy. He left the computer to its work, went back down to the bathroom to freshen himself up as best he could. He made a cup of tea and brought it with him back upstairs. The laptop had finished copying O'Mahoney's disc by this time. He took it out, put it on the desk beside him, inserted a blank disc, and commanded the machine to copy the information onto it. As the machine got to work, he heard the sound of a car with a powerful engine draw up below his windows. He went to look and saw it was Mary O'Mahoney, getting out of a large, lemon convertible with cream leather seats, by far the most expensive-looking car he had seen on the street in all the time he had been living there. She was wearing a black top and matching slacks, and was moving swiftly.

She rang twice on the doorbell as he made his way carefully down the stairs. He had her disc in the envelope in which she had given it to him, and he placed it on a table in the back room before going to answer the door. When he did, O'Mahoney walked straight down the hall and into his back room.

'You gave me a promise,' she said as she passed him.

When they were both in the back room, she was unable to stand still such was her agitation and anger.

'Your word obviously means nothing. I can't believe you did this to me. I don't know what in God's name you think you are going to achieve.'

'I didn't do anything,' he said, closing the door to the hall and then standing with his back to it.

She snorted.

'I don't want to do anything that would jeopardise my settlement. He could tie me up in the courts for the rest of my life. Give me back my disc. And I'm warning you: if one iota of this information gets to anyone I will hold you responsible and make you pay. I will sue you. I will have you sent to jail.'

It was so odd for Christopher to find himself in his house, in such a small room, with an impassioned woman who was all but a stranger to him, talking to him in such a way. Her cheeks were flushed and her hands were shaking. The most surprising aspect of it all was her tone.

'Are you threatening me?'

'Yes I'm threatening you. What planet do you live on? Let me say it again. If anyone anywhere gets any of this information, I will come after you. I will hire the best lawyers in this city. I will lie under oath that you tried to seduce me, that you tried to force yourself on me. I will tell all sorts of lies, do anything I can, to protect what I have. Do you understand? I'm a rich woman and I can pay people to squash you.'

Why, he thought, should he have to put up with this? After all his striving to do good, his renunciation of personal gain, his submission to the Church's desires; why, after all that, had he to stand in his small terraced house listening to this avaricious woman speak to him in such a tone. She felt entitled to speak to him so impolitely and arrogantly because she was rich and he was a man without a penny to his name.

'Get out,' he said.

She looked around the unloved room.

'Believe me, I have no desire to stay here a minute longer than I have to. Now give me the disc.'

He pointed to where it lay on the table with the word Church scrawled on it in block capitals. She picked it up as he opened the door to the hall and stood aside so she could leave.

She paused in the hall and turned to look at him.

'If you've made a copy of this, I swear to you–'

'Get out,' he repeated, louder this time.

She left his front door open. He watched her circle her car, get in, start the engine and drive off without glancing back. Mrs Lacey was at her door and when he walked up to close his, some of her cigarette smoke drifted into the hall and filled him with a sense of nausea.

He decided he would wash and then go to his office in the Archbishop's Palace.

EIGHTEEN

'For I say unto you, I will not drink of the fruit of the vine, until the Kingdom of God shall come.' Christ's words on the night of his Last Supper came to mind as Christopher made his way through the Basin towards Dorset Street. He had an almighty hangover, one of the manifestations of which was a fear that he might trip and topple over. His head was throbbing and he felt curiously light, as if his nervous system had become semi-detached from the meat and bone that formed the rest of his anatomy. There was a sensation of sweating on his forehead, though he was not sure if there was in fact any sweating going on. A mild wind was blowing over the water of the Basin, yet he could still hear the oddly loud sound of the air he was breathing moving in and out through his nostrils. He was, he thought, thoroughly poisoned.

Nevertheless there was an aspect to hangovers that Christopher found interesting. In the same way that his nervous system felt distant from the rest of his body, so too his mind felt more than usually detached from his specific cares. He often found that the mornings after he had consumed too much alcohol were particularly conducive to abstract thought, to the never quite random juxtaposition of the quotidian and the profound, the sacred and the profane, the relevant and the just plain odd. This sense of philosophical detachment, and its associated emphasis on whimsy, was, he often thought, something to which the world should give more attention, because of its capacity to provide not just insight, but comfort and a sense of good cheer.

On the other hand, he knew that a dehydrated brain and shattered nerves were not ideal when trying to make sense of the most likely incomplete and possibly random collection of documents he suspected were on the computer disc that was in his jacket pocket. He was quite possible about to go deep into the world, and it would be better if he had his wits about him.

At a corner on Dorset Street a dust-covered man carrying a large plastic container of water on one shoulder was standing outside a gutted building that was being renovated. Christopher was reminded of a conversation he had had with John about Jesus's last day of freedom before his crucifixion. Jerusalem had been packed to capacity for the feast of the Passover and Jesus had sent Peter and John into the city, instructing them to follow a man they would spot doing the woman's task of carrying a jug of water. They had followed such a man and he had brought them to a furnished room on the upper floor of a building, with a table set so Jesus and his disciples could celebrate the feast of the Passover within the city's walls. Who was the man with the jug, and what was his connection with Jesus? Who had organised it that Jesus and his followers would have a room reserved for them in the thronged city?

'Some follower of Jesus the disciples didn't know about,' John had said. 'It is just a detail, lost in time. What's the point of thinking about it?'

Something about John's tone had made it clear that he did not welcome his friend's invitation for conjecture. Christopher remembered this as he waited at a junction on Dorset Street for the pedestrian lights to change. A bus turned the corner and he stood back to avoid its hot and sooty fumes. The dust-covered man turned to look at him and, as he did so, Christopher spotted the unmistakable signs of a hangover. The man's face had an unhealthy pallor; his skin was curiously dry and his eyes bloodshot. Christopher wondered if his own appearance made it equally obvious how he was feeling. The conspiratorial nod he got from the man just as the lights changed answered Christopher's question.

He crossed the road, walked along by the shops and under the railway bridge, then stopped again to cross Drumcondra Road to the far footpath that ran under the trees and alongside the Archbishop's

Palace walls. On the night of the Last Supper Jesus and his disciples had sat at the table, eaten their Passover meal and washed it down with wine. They had sung hymns. It was the only mention of music in the Gospels. Some day, Christopher thought, he would find out what sort of hymns Jews sang on the eve of the Passover, find out if it was possible to hear the songs that Jesus himself might have sung as the hour of his torment and death drew near.

The grounds of the Archbishop's Palace were empty as Christopher had hoped they would be. There was no sign of Whelan's car and Christopher thought he must be out being interviewed by Nolan. He scanned the grounds for dogs. Sometimes people slipped into the grounds to walk their dogs, even to allow them defecate there. On occasion the dogs were let off their leads to go for a run. When Christopher, with his terror of dogs, found himself in the grounds at the same time as a dog that was off its lead, he would stiffen with worry, while recalling that dogs could sense fear. He would walk purposefully forward with his eyes focused on the middle distance.

Christopher let himself in quietly, made his way through the building to his upstairs office without meeting anyone. He turned on his computer, took off his jacket and sat at his desk as the bulky old PC complained about being woken. The office was a large, almost square room with grey linoleum on the floor and faded yellow wallpaper. There was the table that served as his desk, and some wooden chairs. The furniture was functional and ugly. Metal filing cabinets were lined along one wall, and floor to ceiling shelves stuffed with documents, reports and an eclectic mix of books, filled another. Behind Christopher, as he sat at the large table, was a high sash window that looked out onto the palace grounds and the tall chestnuts, pines and holly trees that grew there. Despite the furniture and the decor, he liked his office, because of its proportions and because of the view out onto the trees.

He arrived in the office at around midday and by the time the light outside had begun to fade, the floor of the room was covered with piles of pages printed from his computer. He was focusing on a Jersey company that had its registered address at the offices of the legal firm in St Helier that O'Mahoney used for most of his offshore business. The firm was known to Christopher because of a connection with a commercial property in the north city that had been left to the Archdiocese some years earlier.

Now Christopher looked again at the file on that bequest. The property had been owned by a Dublin businessman and had been transferred to a Jersey company many years before the bequest. In the weeks prior to the bequest, ownership had been transferred on to another Jersey company and that company had then transferred ownership to the Archdiocese.

Christopher retrieved a copy of the will of the deceased businessman from the Church files. It was a discrete will, dealing solely with the matter of the assets of the Jersey company, and it stated that a separate will had been written in Dublin in relation to the rest of the man's estate.

John had once made a point to Christopher during a discussion on the formation of children that had struck a chord. His friend was strongly of the view that the context or ethos within which actions were carried out was all-important, so that the effect on a child of a lecture on a mathematical problem or a French verb was completely different in a Catholic school, with its emphasis on the implementation of God's will, to that on a child studying in a State school with no religious ethos, where the object was to make the emerging student useful to society, or eminently employable. John had a strong sense of how the context within which a person operates influences what he does, and thereby what he becomes. 'It's a complex loop system,' he would say. 'We become what we do.'

Christopher remembered the conversation as he worked on the disc's files and married them with the files already in his office. He pursued the mortgage registered earlier in relation to the property he was interested in and discovered a link to another property in south Dublin. This led him back to the law firm in St Helier and transfers of ownership involving the south Dublin property. On he went through the clues left in the world of company registers and registries of deeds, trying to establish what it was that the persons who had organised the various transactions had been striving to achieve. His hungover brain produced random musings founded on the facts he was discovering. As his theory developed as to what had happened, he grew more concerned for the moral health of the persons involved.

By the late evening Christopher was convinced that O'Mahoney and his clients were involved in similar transactions to that of the woman whose bequest to the Church had been snaffled by Bishop Finnegan. They had moved the ownership of property and other assets to Jersey to evade paying tax, and the buildings subsequently bequeathed to the Church were portions of those assets – guilt money. Efforts to purchase salvation. He paused to ponder the wonders of the human heart but soon found himself pondering the mysteries of his particular heart. What was it about him that had led to his being a book-keeper, a person who was happiest when alone in his office with his files and his online access to the Companies Registration Office and the Registry of Deeds. If a person became what they did, then what was he?

He stood and paced the room so as to quieten his soul. Then he sat again at his table and resumed his work. He knew as he worked that the determination with which he was willing himself to focus on the task in hand had its source in the agitation he felt as a result of his querying what it was he had become. An hour or more passed and more and more documents were printed, stapled, and dropped onto the office floor. Then when scrolling down through a document he had pulled up on screen, Christopher came across mention of the land near Clontarf which the Church was in the process of selling to Hogan for his Seafront Towers project. He printed out the document, referred to his own files, then went to look again at Land Registry files. There was no reason to doubt what he had found. If he was correct and O'Mahoney had been helping clients bequeath to the Church land and property that had been the subject of elaborate tax evasion, then the parcel of land that was being sold to Hogan had such a provenance.

Further work brought new revelations. One document on the disc indicated that when he was involved in property transactions, including assisting the Church with the handling of bequests, O'Mahoney had charged both the purchaser and the vendor, or in the case of the Church, the donor and the recipient. Photocopied journal entries indicated a large bank balance in O'Mahoney's name in the Jersey branch of an Irish bank which, Christopher presumed, was money the Revenue Commissioners would be interested in being told about. Furthermore, in one or two instances Christopher saw where property owned by deceased clients of O'Mahoney's appeared to end up in O'Mahoney's ownership. Christopher suspected that these properties had been intended for the Church, but that O'Mahoney had been unable to resist the temptation to steal them for himself.

By the time he had come this far in his investigations, all light had gone from the day and Christopher had pulled the blinds on his window. The floor of the office was strewn with documents. Christopher was tired and hungry and his nerves were beginning to champ for alcohol.

He took out his mobile phone and called the Archbishop on his.

'You!' Whelan growled when Christopher introduced himself. 'You have some nerve ringing me today of all days. Did you hear me on the radio?'

While studying his files Christopher had forgotten about Whelan's radio interview.

'I was working.'

'Working! I thought I told you to do nothing, go nowhere. That man Nolan humiliated me in front of the entire nation and I just had to sit in that studio and squirm. My standing – and therefore the standing of the Church among the people – has been terribly damaged because of you. All day we have been receiving telephone calls from the newspapers. Some are asking if I am going to offer my resignation to the Holy Father. And now I pick up the phone and it's you! What the hell do you think you're doing, ringing me today of all days?'

Christopher waited a moment and then told Whelan that he had been looking through documents belonging to O'Mahoney and he thought he might have been robbing property that was intended for the Church. When Whelan interrupted him, he was close to screaming.

'You *think* he might be stealing. Think! Are you mad! What else do you think! What I would like is if you would stop thinking! That you might never again think would be a great relief to me. In fact, let me tell you now, that if it is the last thing I do before I am sent to Bogotá or Khartoum or wherever Rome is likely to send me, I am going to ensure that something is done about you so you cannot cause any more trouble for the Church.'

Whelan paused for breath.

'What are these documents you're talking about?'

Christopher said the documents raised issues to do with the land that was being sold to Hogan, and that he did not think the sale should go ahead until the issues raised were resolved. Without thinking why he was doing so, he also told Whelan that the person who had given him the documents on a confidential basis had sought their return but that he, Christopher, had secretly made copies. When he finished speaking, Whelan did not immediately respond. Christopher could hear the Archbishop breathing heavily through his nose and could imagine his effort to assert self-control. When he did at last speak, it was in a quiet and very controlled way.

'Now you listen to me. You are a bishop of the Church and I am your superior. I am commanding you to destroy those documents and never to mention them again to anyone and never to act on any of the information you may have gathered from your improper examination of those documents. Do you understand? I am *commanding* you. You are a priest and a bishop, subject to sacred duties of obedience to the Church and the Holy Father, and I am commanding you.'

The depth of Whelan's rage was like a coiled beast in the room.

'There is something else,' Christopher said. He recalled the passage from the Gospels where Jesus told his disciples to go and spread the word, and not to worry about what they were going to say. 'For it is not ye that speak, but the Holy Ghost.'

Christopher took a deep breath and spoke.

'I don't believe in God any more.'

Whelan started to cough and choke at the same time.

'What are you talking about?' he asked, when he at last managed to speak.

'I've realised that I don't believe in God,' Christopher said.

'Are you going mad?' Whelan shouted. 'Are you having some sort of nervous episode?'

'No, your Grace,' said Christopher. 'It dawned on me last night. With great clarity. I don't believe in God. I'm not sure exactly when it was that I stopped believing. It's just gone. Completely. My faith I mean. I don't believe any of it. Not one word.'

NINETEEN

CHRISTOPHER DECIDED TO GO HOME. He switched off his computer and packed all the documents he had printed into an old rucksack of his that was lying in a corner of the room. The bag was heavy and he struggled to get it onto his shoulders. He paused at the door on his way out, looked long at the room where he had spent so much time in the service of an institution he would now have to leave.

He wondered if he had been foolish to reveal his loss of faith to Whelan. There were probably hundreds of priests in the Church who no longer believed, kept their secret to themselves, and continued to give comfort to their parishioners and to avail of the opportunity the Church provided for other good works.

What did it matter, he thought, what he believed?

Everything, he answered himself.

He shifted the bag on his shoulders, then turned off the light for the last time.

'Everything,' he said to the darkness, and closed the door.

Christopher walked down the wide stairs to the spacious empty lobby dominated by a statue of Jesus displaying his Sacred Heart. He opened the well-hung wooden door, closed it gently behind him and ensured that the lock had caught. The grounds were pitch black save for some lights showing the way along the path to the gates, and there was an invigorating freshness in the air. He could feel the desire for a drink in every organ, muscle and nerve of his body. To hell with that, he thought. I will have to find better things to do.

The path to the gates was lined with flowerbeds and low bushes. He set off along it, thinking of how he was walking out of his old life, that he would pass through the gates and into a future he could not imagine. The act of speaking to Whelan had clarified his new position in his own mind, and the enormity of what had occurred. Belief that had lasted a lifetime had simply disappeared. What traces would it leave? What stars in the night sky would he now use to guide him? More than ever before, and in a way that was so new for him, he felt entirely alone.

His future was his to create, he was thinking, but then a large dog appeared from the low bushes. It was a muscular dog, a light-brown mongrel with the genes, Christopher thought, of a Labrador but also those of a pitbull or some such fighting breed. He let out a soft cry of fright and pulled back, startling the dog as he did so. The brute began to snarl, displaying an armoury of white teeth embedded in blood-red gums. There was no sign of any owner, indeed of anyone at all in the palace grounds. This is it, Christopher thought. I am about to encounter Hell.

But then, to his own great surprise, he lifted the heavy sack of documents from his shoulder, held it momentarily at full arms' stretch above him, and brought it down hard and sideways against the dog's head. He felt the thump of the load collide with the beast's skull, and saw how the heft of the bag knocked the animal's head sharply to its right. He thought he heard a cracking sound, but he wasn't sure. Still without forethought, he lifted the sack again and held it over the animal's head in preparation for a second blow. The dog, however, had fallen on its side and was lying with its mouth open and the end of its impossibly long tongue resting on the tarmac. Christopher watched as its dark eyes glazed over and its expression changed. Christopher's heart was thumping, his blood racing through his veins; he was filled with a sense of vanquished fear and growing elation. The once dreaded monster seemed deep inside itself now, stunned by how suddenly its quota of days had come to an end. There was a trickle of blood coming from its mouth, and its gums were growing pale. Christopher lowered the sack and looked around to see if his murderous act had been witnessed.

Just outside the gates, standing as if they had been watching him, were the shadows of two men. The palace grounds were otherwise empty, and the night was curiously still. Because they were making no effort to move towards him, Christopher suspected that the men were not the dog's owners. He shouldered his bag of documents and stepped over the dying brute. The shadows who had been watching him disappeared. When he reached the gates and passed through them, there was no sign of the two men. No one called after him from the palace grounds. Nervous, though still filled with a sense of manly exultation and strength, Christopher set off down Lower Drumcondra Road towards home.

But the idea of going home reminded him of the declaration he had made to Whelan and the realisation dawned that soon he would have to leave his terraced house in Broadstone and the neighbours he had come to know. This idea in turn made him feel a desire to go to his childhood home, and sit once again in its peaceful front room with his elderly mother. He turned around to walk back in the direction from which he had just come and, as he did so, he spotted the two men he had seen earlier at the palace gates. They were skulking along under the tall trees, on the grass that grew between the elevated footpath and the low railings that lined the roadside. It seemed to Christopher that they had been following him, and had been surprised by his sudden reversal of direction. He could see they were adults, stocky, with the bearing of men who spent time in the gym, working on their muscles. Both were wearing woollen hats, zipped up jackets that came to their waists, and bright running shoes that, Christopher thought, should not be worn by people intent on slyly stalking people along darkened thoroughfares.

It was almost by way of acknowledging that they had been caught that the two men climbed over the low railings that marked the kerbside, and negotiated their way through the traffic to the other side of the road. When they got to the other side, they clambered over the low railings there and stopped among the trees and the shadows. They stood there, watching him, unconcerned that their reconnaissance was now itself being observed. Christopher was confused by his discovery that he was being followed, but was also still filled with the excitement of his recent successful act of violence. Thinking that he did not want to lead these men towards his mother's house, he walked purposefully to the edge of the road and flagged a taxi he had spotted heading towards the city centre. The car pulled over and, as Christopher opened its near rear door, he saw that the two men on the other side of the road had started towards him and then stopped, recognising that there was nothing they could do to prevent their quarry's escape. Christopher sat in the back of the taxi and asked the driver to take him into town. The driver, who was African, pulled out into the traffic. When the car was drawing close to Eccles Street and Christopher was sure that he had not been followed, he told the driver he had changed his mind, and asked to be taken back to Glasnevin.

His mother was in the front room, just as he had expected, watching a soap opera on television, while, in the kitchen, the radio was playing the *Valse Triste* by Sibelius.

He stood at the door into the sitting room.

'Hi. I was down in my office and I thought I'd just call in for a minute and see how you are.'

'Well I'm still here,' she said, looking away from the screen for only the briefest of glances.

He said he would go to the bathroom. There, he washed his face, then sat on the edge of the loo, thinking of the dog and the two men who had witnessed his brutal act. They had not been burglars waiting for him to leave the Archbishop's Palace, because they had followed him as he had walked away. They had not sought to remonstrate with him for killing the dog. He wondered for a while as to why they had decided to follow him, then decided that thinking about it further would get him nowhere.

In the kitchen he turned off the radio, tidied away a soup bowl and cup and saucer his mother had left on the draining board. When he went up to join her, her programme had ended and she had used the remote control to turn down the volume. He sat on the sofa close to her armchair.

'I heard Archbishop Whelan on the radio this morning,' she said, looking at the silenced advertisements playing on the TV screen. 'I wasn't very impressed.'

'I'm not the Archbishop's favourite bishop at the moment.'

'That doesn't surprise me,' she answered, chuckling.

'And now I have come across new information that I think is going to cause fresh trouble.'

He had made it clear from his tone that something of importance was involved, and was surprised that her response was to be even more amused.

'You were always a great one for information. God, you used to bore us to death sometimes when you were young, reeling off yards of information about this, that or the other, and us trying to have a conversation with you. You've never changed.'

He decided not to be distracted.

'You always taught me to do what I believed was right.'

'Yes,' she said, her tone changed to one of regret. 'Sometimes I worry that we said that to you too often.'

'What do you mean, Mammy?'

'Well, when you were a child you were always trying to be good, Christopher. My mother and father were always at me to be good, and I tried to be. It was the same with your father and his parents. We were both brought up to be good, and we tried to do the same with you. But sometimes I regret that we didn't encourage you to challenge the idea more. To find out about life for yourself. And that we didn't do more ourselves to discover our bad sides.'

Christopher wasn't sure where she was going with the conversation, and didn't know how to respond. He was unused to articulated intimacy. To what sort of badness, he wondered, was she referring? He feared greatly that it might be to do with sex. If she started to talk about that, he decided, he would leave the room.

She turned and looked at him with unusual intensity. There were the hints of tears in her eyes.

'I'm afraid that we didn't treat you fairly...didn't give you enough room. We let you try to please us when we should have let you go out in the world and become whatever it was you wanted to be. People need to find out what it is they want, what it is they are. There's no harm in healthy selfishness. And we all need to know about our bad sides. I'm not saying there is anything wrong with being good, or that we should not try to be good. But you shouldn't find yourself, at the end of your days, regretting all you haven't done, and realising it is too late now – your time is gone.'

'Is that how you feel, Mammy?'

'No, Christopher. I'm not talking about me, though maybe I do feel that way a little, to be honest. But we had a good marriage, and were blessed with you. All I had ever wanted was children, and I'd thought I'd never have them, and then you came along. There's nothing makes you appreciate something as much as being frightened that you'll never have it.'

She moved her hand as if checking were there tears on her cheek.

'It is more that I'm frightened it will be you. That you will end up wishing you'd looked out for yourself more.'

He wanted to walk over and kiss her on the forehead. He felt a gentleness and gratitude for her existence similar to that he had felt when he had kissed Simone's scalp during their dance together in her kitchen. The sense of manliness he had experienced during his encounter with the dog was still with him, and now here he was confronted with being loved. He sensed how rich life could be, but he remained sitting where he was on the sofa.

'Mammy,' he said, 'I wanted to ask you to make a new will and to leave the house to me. This house. I've always loved it. Would you mind?'

'Is that allowed?'

'It will be. Something's happened.'

She tightened her grip on her chair and he noted her white knuckles against her paper-thin, liver-spotted-covered skin.

'Don't be alarmed. It's nothing bad. At least I don't think so.'

He could see anxiety in her eyes.

'Mammy, I don't believe in God any more.'

At first she appeared puzzled by his words but then she sat back in her chair and the shaking of her chin ceased. She thought about what he had said, and then, to his astonishment, she began to laugh.

'Well, that's a gallery! Jesus you're something. Have you told Whelan?'

'Just now. Over the phone. He wants to meet me tomorrow.'

'I'll say he does.'

She rested her head on the back of her chair and continued to laugh. She seemed happy. Soon he joined in and so the two of them found themselves sitting in front of the silent TV laughing at the fact that he no longer believed in God. The oddness of the scene in itself contributed to Christopher's amusement.

'You don't mind?'

'To tell you the truth, Christopher, I think I'm delighted.'

When he had come home from university one day to tell her he wanted to become a priest, she had made him sit down on the same sofa and had questioned him closely. He couldn't recall what it was she had said but he remembered clearly her obvious concern about what he had chosen to do with his life.

'I'm going to resign. I am going to leave the Church altogether.'

'You could stay on if you wanted. There's lots of them, I'd say, if you pinned them up against the wall, would admit that they don't believe.'

'Do you, Mammy?'

'If I was younger,' she said, 'I might stop believing. But now I feel, what's the point? I might as well keep going. And I get some comfort from my prayers.'

They sat comfortably in silence. He admired her and felt very close to her.

'Is there something else?' she said then, her eyebrows arched in expectation of some gossip. 'Is there a woman?'

He told her there might be. He didn't know her very well. They had eaten dinner together in her house recently, and he liked her. He thought there was a chance she might like him. 'I'm not sure. I'm not very well versed in these matters.'

'You still have time to learn. Not a lot, but maybe enough if you get on with it.'

She lifted the remote and the TV screen went dark. The conversation and the laughter, he thought, had tired her.

'You think you have lots of time,' she said. 'And then you find you don't.'

TWENTY

CHRISTOPHER LINGERED IN THE sitting room after his mother had gone to bed, remembering his childhood days there, the sound of his father coming in the gate, of his mother chastising some unfortunate child at the piano in the dining room. On Sundays they had their dinner in that room, a few hours after morning mass, his aproned father handing plates piled with roast meat in through the hatch from the kitchen, the table set with napkins and candlesticks and, sometimes, a vase of wild flowers from the lane. Even how they ate together was a form of moral education.

He had been lonely all his life, including during his childhood, but when he had been living in that house, it had been a home and he had been swathed in love. Cocooned. When he had walked in the garden gate and up the steps to the door, he had felt certain that he was in the presence of an almost absolute love.

Maybe, he thought, what people do is to seek to construct their lives so that they have what they need to be happy. Maybe they focus on that, and act with determination. Straightaway he knew that it would be a shallow and dangerous guiding principle for a person trying to negotiate the hazards of existence. Yet he was not sure what else there was in a godless universe.

When he left the house he closed the gate gently, walked in the dark down Washerwoman's Hill and across the bridge that spanned the rushing, tinselly-sounding Tolka. He turned left into Botanic Avenue and when he got to the junction with Mobhi Road, he stood there and flagged down the first taxi that came. The young driver was from

127

Poland and spoke English well, but had no knowledge of the city. Christopher spelled out his address and the man typed the words into his satellite navigator before starting to drive. He had, he explained, come to Dublin two weeks earlier. When customers took him out to the west of the city, where so much housing had been built in recent years, the satnav often did not recognise the addresses. Frequently, after he dropped off such customers, he got lost.

The navigator did not know that some of the streets near where Christopher lived had bollards blocking cars' access to his street. The Polish man drove into one such street before Christopher noticed. The young man offered to turn off his taxi meter and drive Christopher to his house by another route, but Christopher told him not to bother, that it was a lovely night for a short walk.

There wasn't another soul walking on Canal Bank Terrace. No lights glowed in any of the large houses that looked out towards the Basin. Some of the people in those houses believed they slept in a God-created universe, their every dream and act known to an almighty Father. But Christopher didn't believe that any longer, and no one but he knew his secret thoughts and solitary actions. Neither he nor anyone else knew what would transpire in his life over the coming days, months and years: save that his beloved mother would one day die; and that some time afterwards he would follow her.

These were the thoughts that were in his mind when he noticed shadows at the end of his street, not far from the door of his home. Two men were standing beside a parked car, one of them smoking a cigarette. It struck Christopher that they were very like the two men who had been waiting outside the Archbishop's Palace earlier that evening.

He walked down the street on the pavement opposite the one where the men were waiting, keeping close to the wall. His heart was thumping, but he did not consider turning. They were not talking. They were simply standing by their car, keeping watch on the empty street, with an air of bored ease that indicated they had been doing so for some time. There was, Christopher noted, a third man sitting at the wheel of the car.

The men were standing about four houses down from his, on the far side of the narrow street. Christopher stopped in the shadows and wondered what he should do. For once he found himself wishing that Mrs Lacey was standing at her door, smoking a cigarette, noticing everything. But no lights showed in any of the houses. Everyone was sleeping except Christopher and the waiting men farther up the road.

Then a car turned into the street, coming from the same end as Christopher. It was a large four-wheel drive, its headlights blazing bright. Christopher ducked down behind one of the parked cars that lined the narrow street on both sides and, once the slow-moving four-wheel drive came level with him, he hurried along the pavement just behind it, trusting that its headlights would stop the men at the far end of the street from seeing him. He came to his door, slipped the key in the lock, and entered the house as the large car was slowly rounding the tight corner near where the men were standing. He closed the door as gently as he could, stood in the hall listening. All he heard was the sound of his own troubled breathing. After shoving home a bolt he rarely used, and making sure the latch was locked, he went upstairs in his stockinged feet, in the darkness. He approached the upstairs front room window and looked carefully out. The men were still there, maintaining their vigil, seemingly bored.

In bed, troubled by the presence of the men outside but also by his desire for alcohol, Christopher found it hard to sleep. He forgot for a time about the men and reviewed again the conversation he had had with his mother. This in turn led him to recall what Simone had said about how choosing one possibility in life involved a decision to forego another. He thought of how, because people live only once, they were limited in what they could know about their choices. A person's ability to comment on the quality of a cup of coffee was limited if it was the only coffee they had ever tasted. Likewise with life; the life chosen could not be compared with the alternative life forgone, and people were therefore constrained as to what they could say about the effects of the choices they had made. All a person could do, he thought, was strive. He hoped his mother had not conceded too easily. It was not too late, he decided, for him to seek fulfilment. The search for peace could come later.

Another thought crossed his mind before he fell asleep. His mother had always said goodness had to be honest. It was one of her central philosophies, something she also said about music, though he wasn't quite so sure what she meant in that regard. Good playing had to be honest, she would say. He wondered who had implanted this concept of honesty in her soul. Perhaps her parents, just as the idea had been planted in him by her. It was one of the central messages Jesus had preached. Maybe that was so because it was an idea known to almost everyone. Perhaps the central messages of Jesus were at one and the same time powerful and obvious. Trite even. He found himself smiling at that idea as he slipped into sleep, in the quiet, and the darkness.

TWENTY-ONE

THE PERSISTENT SHRILL RINGING OF his doorbell woke Christopher from the depths of sleep. The light outside his window was that of early dawn. He remembered the men and went to the front of the house to peek from the edge of one of the windows onto the street below. There were two cars now. He could see men sitting inside the silver saloon which was still parked where it had been the night before. Directly underneath him, Christopher could see the roof of a very large black Mercedes Benz, and the crown of the head of the man who had obviously just stepped back from having one of his fingers pressed against Christopher's doorbell. The car, and something about the man's military bearing, caused Christopher to decide he was not a threat.

He descended the stairs and opened the door that went from the downstairs room to the hallway. 'One minute!' he shouted. He dressed quickly, threw some water over his face, noting while he was doing so how he could already feel the benefits of his abstinence from alcohol.

The man outside the door was as tall as Christopher, better built, had his hair cut in a short back and sides, and seemed ill at ease in his suit, tie, and polished black leather shoes. Mrs Lacey was at her door in her pink eiderdown dressing gown and large fluffy slippers, a half-smoked cigarette in her hand.

'Good morning, your Grace,' she said when Christopher appeared. 'You're getting very classy callers these days.'

The man stepped forward and introduced himself while taking a wallet from his inside jacket pocket.

'Detective Sergeant Bill Flynn, your Grace. I'm one of the Taoiseach's drivers. He sent me to bring you to Government Buildings, for a meeting.'

'First I heard of it,' said Christopher.

The detective sergeant didn't respond. The silver car across the road had started up its engine as soon as Christopher had opened his door, and now it began to drive slowly away. A muscled, short-haired man wearing a leather sports jacket was sitting in the back seat and Christopher made eye-contact with him as the car passed. The man's stare was cold and hard, his scowl steeped in menace.

'You'd better put on some shoes if you're meeting the fecking Taoiseach,' said Mrs Lacey, looking down at Christopher's naked feet.

'Just give me a minute,' Christopher said to the detective sergeant.

Christopher put on a clean pair of black slacks and a fresh black shirt. Without noticing he was doing so, he put on his Roman collar. When putting on his jacket, he checked that the disc containing the documents Mary O'Mahoney had given him was still in the inside pocket. He fetched the rucksack of documents he had put in the wardrobe the night before and brought it out to his backyard. He stood up on the flowerbed to look over the wall to Mrs Lacey's. She was standing in her kitchenette taking her pills. He got her attention by hissing and she came outside and stood beside him on the other side of the wall.

'Will you mind this for me? It's heavy.'

He lowered the sack down onto her side of the wall. 'They're just property deeds and the like. But mind them for me.'

'You're up to something, you devil you.'

'Thanks,' he said. He went back into his kitchen and locked the door behind him.

Christopher sat in the back seat of the Mercedes and the garda drove him through the empty, early morning city. Beside Christopher on the car seat was a copy of an evening newspaper from the day before, and some print-outs of pages from news websites. The edge of a discarded crisp packet was just visible on the floor under the front passenger seat. The car purred its way through the streets, an effective symbol, not of money, but of power.

The iron gates at Government Buildings opened automatically as the car approached. They circled a fountain and drew up beside the steps to the building's main entrance. Before he could act, the detective was out of the car and opening Christopher's door. The detective walked up the steps and Christopher followed. A porter activated the automatic lock to allow them enter and they made their way through a hallway flagged with black and white tiles, then up a luxuriously carpeted flight of stairs, dominated by a large, stained-glass window that bathed the scene with coloured light.

On an upper floor Christopher followed the detective along a corridor with windows to the left looking back out onto the fountain and the gates and the Georgian buildings on the opposite site of Upper Merrion Street. On one of the doors on the right Christopher noticed the title Attorney General. Examples of contemporary Irish art decorated the walls between the doors. They stopped outside a door near the end of the corridor and the detective knocked gently before immediately entering and inviting Christopher to follow him. It was a large room in which the antique mahogany furniture glowed, the desktops were ordered and in the main clear, and the atmosphere was heavy with the aura of waiting. A woman with short dyed-blonde hair and wearing a dark suit was sitting at one of the desks drinking tea from a dainty white teacup and saucer. The small milk jug beside her appeared to be pure silver. She looked up from her newspaper and smiled at the detective as if they were party to some wry observation or joke. The antique clock on the wall above her gave the time as seven twenty.

Christopher was told where to sit. The woman rose, knocked on a door, opened it slightly and leaned in.

'He's here,' she said, addressing someone in the room beyond.

There was no response. The woman leaned back and closed the door gently as she did so, then returned to her desk and her newspaper. The detective took a cup from a tray on a sideboard and poured himself tea, sat at another mahogany desk and began to browse through a newspaper. Christopher was offered neither information nor tea.

It was gone half past seven when a buzzer sounded on the woman's desk. She promptly rose and went and opened the door to the Taoiseach's office.

'You can go in now,' she said to Christopher, as if he was in a doctor's surgery.

Brady was sitting behind a large L-shaped desk reading through some documents and did not look up as Christopher entered. The door closed behind him. There was no one else in the room. Newspapers were scattered on the floor behind and beside Brady's desk. A torn page was scrunched up in a ball and was resting on the floor on the far side of the room. The lime wallpaper was interrupted by the occasional framed photograph or painting, including one over the marble mantelpiece showing the profile of one of the leaders of the 1916 Rising, Patrick Pearse.

On one side of Brady's desk, beside a large and old-fashioned computer, there was a tray containing what looked to be the remains of a large fried breakfast. On the plate there was congealed egg, the smears from baked beans in tomato sauce, rasher rinds, and the crusts of some slices of toast. A cup similar to the ones Christopher had seen outside sat on top of a headline Brady had presumably torn from one of the newspapers. The Taoiseach let out a long, pained sigh, collected the A4 pages he had been perusing and knocked them into a neat bundle before putting them on the floor beside him. He sat back in his chair and only then raised his eyes to Christopher.

'Who the fuck do you think you are?'

The venom and the use of the curse word shocked Christopher, though he also thought that the effect was probably intended. Brady was a picture of suppressed violence, his face red, scrunched. Christopher was at a loss for words.

'What's your fucking game?'

'I'm sorry?'

The response appeared to enrage Brady even further.

'Look, I'm a busy man. I've got a country to run. Everywhere I go people are whingeing about this and that and fucking everything. Ten years ago we had an average per capita income that was below 75 per cent of the western EU average, now we're about 120 per cent. Our debt to GDP ratio is the lowest in Europe. So are our taxes. No one is better off than us, other than the fucking Luxembourgers, and there's only about twelve of them. Yet all I get, morning, noon and night, is fucking whingeing and moaning and nah-nah-nah; what about fucking him? – He's getting more than I get, it's not fair. Bollix, bollix, bollix. A shower of ungrateful, whingeing cunts.'

Brady tore a page from a newspaper and rolled it violently into a ball before throwing it towards Christopher, who dodged to one side so that it passed him and bounced dully off the wall behind. He didn't have time to consider whether or not Brady had been trying to hit him before the rant resumed.

'More is never enough. No. Everyone wants to be the fucking richest, have one over on everyone else. What about me? I've burst my fucking arse to make this country what it is today, sacrificed my time with my family, my health. I could have made millions if I'd gone into business, could be flying around in my own helicopter instead of some old crock owned by the fucking army. But no, I gave it all up to serve the country. Everywhere I go they want to shake your hand and the women want to kiss you – they'd show you their tits if you'd let them – but the minute you turn your back, the fucking knives are out, the fucking tongues start wagging, the lies and the shit start to fly. Two minutes down the road and you're the biggest fucking bollix since Cromwell.'

Brady stood up. The menace in the room felt so tangible Christopher imagined the walls were bulging in their effort to accommodate it. The Taoiseach was radiating rage. He had his jacket off and Christopher could see the corpulent belly that had pushed the front bibs of his white shirt out of his trousers so they hung down over his flies. Surely the Taoiseach of the day wasn't going to come round his desk and attack a bishop in Government Buildings? Such things didn't happen, Christopher told himself. But he wasn't entirely convinced.

Brady paused at the side of his desk.

'And now I have to deal with fucking you! A fucking bishop! What the fuck do you want to be interfering in business for, trying to cause trouble, stop a building project that will create literally hundreds of jobs and give a boost to the economy when all the fucking cribbers are saying it's going to go down the tubes? Down the fucking tubes! There are more people employed in Ireland than there have been since the Famine!'

He paused to catch his breath. His nose had turned from red to purple, as had the skin on his fleshy cheeks. His eyes, watering now under his hard-haired eyebrows, never left Christopher's, reminding him of the staring games he had seen boys play in his childhood, of the ruffians you might meet on the street who would ask you what you were looking at while fixing you with a demented, threatening stare, inviting you to respond.

'So what's your angle? I want you to tell me now. What's your game?'

Christopher's heart was thumping and his palms were sweating. He remembered that there was a detective sergeant on the other side of the door but he also wondered where his loyalties might lie. No doubt elsewhere in the building there were members of some elite army unit or of the military police. If he threw a chair through a window, surely they would come rushing in, pull Brady off him, bring any violence that might have erupted to an end.

'I'm not sure what you're talking about.'

Brady kept eyeballing him. Was this all a charade, Christopher wondered, part of Brady's armoury, his modus operandi?

'I'm talking about Buzzie Hogan's Seafront project, you gobshite. The deal you're supposed to sign so it can go ahead, the trouble you're causing to a development that could create hundreds of jobs, a project that I've twisted myself inside out to get to this stage. I had to fight half the fucking civil servants in the country, put up with acres of shite from bastards in the papers who earn more than I do for all the time cribbing and criticising and whingeing about what others are doing while they themselves do nothing. That's what I'm talking about!'

Since the detective sergeant had introduced himself, Christopher had assumed the summons to Brady's office was in some way connected with Hogan's project, though he had also, and at the same time, told himself that it could not be so.

'I think the land the Church owns may have been part of an estate on which an amount of tax is due. I may have discovered serious tax fraud.'

At first Brady didn't respond. He breathed noisily through his nostrils. The thought crossed Christopher's mind that soon, within a decade, say, Brady's health difficulties would be chronic. Or that perhaps, by then, he would be already dead, the victim of a sudden heart attack brought on by an outbreak of rage.

'Listen to me, you,' said Brady. 'That's none of your fucking business. I have the Revenue Commissioners on to me every day of the week telling me where they think money is hidden. If they had their way, they'd be searching under everyone's fucking mattress before we all went to bed at night. I don't want to be hearing that sort of shite from the Church as well. You stick to telling old ladies not to be thinking about their gees. Do you hear me? I don't know what your fucking game is, but I run this fucking country. I *control* it. Not you. Not your fucking Church. *Me.* Don't you think for a minute I'm going to let some half-arsed shit like you come along and cause me grief. I'll fucking flatten you. I'll fuck you and your Church. You fuckers are in here every day, looking for this, that or the other. You're the biggest whingers of the lot. Church-state fucking relations. The fucking poor. You and your Church will get nothing but grief if you cross me, do you hear? I'll take your fucking schools off youse, your hospitals, tax your fucking Roman collars, seize the loot you're always swindling out of old dears.'

'I'm going to be resigning as a bishop. I'm leaving the Church.'

'What?'

Any red that was left in Brady's face now disappeared. His entire visage took on an unhealthy purple hue. Beads of sweat appeared on his temples and on the sides of his bulging nose.

'I'm leaving the Church,' Christopher repeated, conscious that his calm tone was fuelling Brady's rage.

Taking his eyes off Christopher, Brady leaned forward and rested his two fists on his desk. A bead of what Christopher imagined to be fatty sweat dripped from the tip of his nose onto the green-leathered surface of the desk. Brady was shaking in a way that Christopher thought might indicate a difficulty with blood sugar levels as well as nerves. Christopher himself sometimes shook when he was very hung-over and had forgotten to eat. There was something tragic, he reflected, about people who tried so hard but whose motives were not rooted in love. Success kept slipping off the fork just as it neared their tongue.

'I've realised,' continued Christopher, remembering his slaying of the dog and feeling that he, now, was in control, 'that I no longer believe in God.'

It was obvious that Brady was at a complete loss. There was a long silence as he tried to gather the strength for a new offensive. Christopher waited, savouring his moment of cruelty.

'You'll never work in this town,' Brady said. 'Never earn a fucking penny. I'll see to that. And every fucking penny someone might give you will be taken from you by the Revenue. I'll see to that too. You'll be sleeping on the fucking streets and the guards will move you on. Every now and then, when no one is around to help you, someone will kick the shit out of you. No one will ever help you. You'll have nothing. You'll be in the gutter. You'll die in the fucking gutter.'

Even as Brady spoke, it was clear that the threats were just so much air. All that remained, now, was to play out the game, the outcome of which had already been decided. Brady moved away from his desk, approached so close to Christopher that Christopher could smell his breakfast from his breath, the faint odour of last night's alcohol from his pores. When he spoke, he was whispering, and his tone was almost kindly.

'Listen to me. This is going to happen. One way or the other. You have no idea who you are putting yourself up against. No idea.'

He turned around then and pushed a button on his desk. He tucked in the ends of his shirt as he walked to behind his desk. He took his jacket off the back of his chair and buttoned it over his enormous stomach. The door opened behind Christopher and when he looked around the woman with blonde hair was waiting, a leather folder of papers cradled in one arm, her gaze towards the floor. Brady walked past Christopher as if he wasn't there and through the doorway, to be followed immediately by the woman. The door was left open so Christopher could see how Brady, walking fast, was followed out into the corridor by the woman and the detective who drove his car. A second woman appeared at the door and stood there, waiting for Christopher to leave, which he did. She saw him out into the corridor and closed the door behind him. No words were exchanged.

Christopher descended the stairs and let himself out through the main doors of Government Buildings, walked around the fountain and out through the gates past the soldiers who gave him a friendly nod. It was soon after eight and his morning lay empty before him. He thought of how he would be no longer attending or saying mass. He would have to find something new to do.

TWENTY-TWO

CHRISTOPHER WALKED ALONG THE north side of St Stephen's Green to Grafton Street. A newsagent's was open on the corner and a small, takeaway coffee outlet just beyond that. Otherwise all the outlets he could see on what had become one of Europe's most expensive streets in terms of commercial rent were still closed for business. Even money sometimes took its ease.

He turned into Chatham Street, walked towards the conservatory he had often visited with his mother when she taught there and which he had attended during his brief musical education. Despite his lack of success as a music student, it remained one of his favourite buildings in the city, by reason of its function. He loved the way you might hear students practising scales as you passed an open window; wind and string instruments, people working on their singing. It served as a welcome alternative to the shop windows displaying their wares, the false promises of the omnipresent consumer culture.

The sky was clear and the morning had the atmosphere of a day that was going to be unseasonably warm. A young man putting tables and chairs outside a café on the corner greeted Christopher with a surprising level of friendliness.

'Beautiful day, Father.'

'Brilliant,' said Christopher, thinking he would have to get himself some new clothes. 'Good for the soul.'

He turned the corner and walked down South William Street. He passed some restaurants, a hairdresser's, a shop selling sex toys. On the opposite side of the street was a shop window that had been put into a Georgian building in which there were plastic models sporting tight black plastic clothes and masks. One was holding a whip. The gate in the building's metal fence leading to its basement steps was open and a small queue of young women was standing there, sipping on hot takeaway drinks and smoking cigarettes. Christopher crossed the street to see what was going on.

The queue went down the steps to the basement door over which was a sign advertising the services of a fortune-teller and tarot card reader. The door appeared to be closed.

'Is this a queue for the fortune-teller?' he asked the young woman at the end of the queue.

Noting his Roman collar and making no effort to conceal her dislike and suspicion, she pulled on her cigarette and sipped at her hot drink, all the time huddled and shivering as if she was cold.

'What's it to you?'

The thoughts that came to his mind about human nature and the search for meaning did not seem appropriate.

She looked away up the street, down at his feet, anywhere but into his eyes.

'Do you really believe in fortune-tellers?' he asked.

'One charlatan is as good as the next if you ask me.'

'Yes, but why do you need charlatans at all?'

'Do us a favour, will you? Get lost.'

The narrow lane alongside Clarendon Street Church was busy with mass-goers and people going to work. A young woman wearing a woollen hat was playing early English music on a fat black recorder. At the end of the lane Christopher turned back up Grafton Street and went into the shop on the corner to buy some newspapers. Outside the café on the corner of Chatham Street he sat on a chair that was being warmed by the early morning sun. The young man who had greeted him earlier appeared and Christopher asked for orange juice, a cooked breakfast with no egg, and coffee.

'Not a bother,' said the young man.

All the newspapers gave extensive coverage to Whelan's performance on the radio the previous day. Most of it was dismissive. There was, commentators maintained, a crisis in society and just when it was most in need of moral leadership, the Church was proving unable to step up to the mark. It too, the commentators said, had lost its way.

There were numerous pictures of Brady in the newspapers and in each one he was either smiling or looking as if he had the weight of the nation on his shoulders. Christopher wondered which of the political reports had been the ones Brady had torn out and thrown across his office floor, what headline it was he had seen carefully torn from the newspaper and secured under Brady's breakfast teacup.

The business sections of the newspapers had reports of how a syndicate of Irish investors had just purchased a European property portfolio worth hundreds of millions of euro. But there were also reports about the extent of the exposure of the Irish banks to the Irish property market, and consideration of the solidity of that market's values. In one paper there was a picture of Buzzie Hogan standing outside an office development he had just completed, clutching a glass of champagne and grinning with unashamed smugness and delight. The accompanying report said some developers had been called to a series of crisis meetings with their bankers that week, with one unnamed source being quoted as confirming the story, and spokesmen for a range of developers, including Hogan, stating firmly that no such meetings had occurred.

There was very little information in the report, which seemed to Christopher to be written with a half-acknowledgement that what was being printed was as much rumour as news. He presumed that Simone was in London attending just such a meeting.

When Christopher looked up from his newspaper, he was shocked to see that the muscled man with the leather jacket who had been in the car outside his house that morning was in the process of sitting down at a table at the far end of the café terrace. Christopher watched as the friendly young waiter approached and the man stayed the hand that was bringing a lighter towards the unlit cigarette he had in his mouth and gruffly ordered a coffee. Christopher quickly looked away and buried his face low in his newspaper.

He finished his meal and drained his coffee, put the money for his breakfast on the table and stood up and left, leaving the newspapers behind him and walking quickly around the corner onto South William Street. The queue for the fortune-teller was longer now, the woman he had spoken with nowhere to be seen. He retraced his steps from earlier but crossed Grafton Street when he got to it and went down South Anne Street, all without looking back to see if he was being followed. Walking down Duke Lane, he saw a young man pulling up the shutters on a clothes shop and he asked if he was open.

'Not really,' the man said. 'But if you want to come in, fire ahead.'

Christopher went down to the basement. He selected a pair of jeans and a thick grey t-shirt. He told the man he would buy them but wanted to wear them straightaway.

'Grand,' the man said.

Christopher changed in a small curtained stall and brought the tags that had been on the clothes to the till. It was only then he realised how expensive they were.

'For a t-shirt and a pair of jeans?'

'They're both top brands,' the man said, as if that was an explanation.

Christopher paid using his bank card. He left, carrying his trousers and priest's shirt inside an unnecessarily large paper bag bearing the shop's name.

As he walked past Lemon Street, the man with the leather jacket stepped out of a doorway and blocked his way.

'Good morning, your G-g-grace,' he said, his face so close Christopher could smell his foul nicotined breath. He touched his fingertips off Christopher's new t-shirt. 'Trying to m-m-melt into the crowd are we?'

Two similarly menacing figures appeared on either side of Christopher, leering rather than smiling.

'What do you want?' Christopher asked. 'Why are you following me?'

The man with the leather jacket stepped in even closer. Christopher found himself looking at the black facial hair that sprouted from his skin, the stained grooves on his teeth.

'We're just making sure you don't get into any trouble. Our job is to make sure that nobody gets h-h-hurt.'

He hissed the last word into Christopher's right ear. Christopher looked over the man's shoulder and saw two uniformed guards walking past the junction where Duke Lane met Duke Street.

'Guards!' he shouted, stepping past the three startled men and heading down the laneway. 'Guards!'

The two guards stopped, turned and began walking unhurriedly towards Christopher.

'Guards', he said again loudly, wishing he was still in his clerical clothes.

They were young, smaller than he was, wearing protective vests to shield them from knife attacks. As he started his explanation, Christopher turned to point to the three men who had been following him, and saw that they had disappeared. A man standing in the lane was watching him closely, but Christopher wasn't sure whether or not he was one of the group that had been menacing him.

'What's the problem?' asked one of the two guards.

'There were three men. One of them, in a black leather jacket, threatened me.'

'Why would he do that?' asked the second garda.

Christopher thought of the story he would have to tell, the priest's clothing in his oversized shopping bag, the oddness of the whole affair.

'He just came up to me and threatened to hurt me,' said Christopher. 'I saw you and I called for you, and when I walked towards you, they disappeared.'

The first garda who had spoken took out his notebook and asked Christopher if he could describe the three men. Christopher said he couldn't and now that they were gone, it hardly mattered. He thanked the guards and walked quickly towards Dawson Street, where he got into one of the taxis waiting in a rank there. He gave the driver his home address. As the car pulled away, Christopher looked behind but could see no sign of the man with the black leather jacket.

When Christopher let himself into his house, it was immediately apparent that it had been broken into and searched. In every room the furniture had been moved, drawers opened, bookshelves and CD shelves emptied. Whoever had searched the house had done so methodically and most probably quietly. The only items that he noticed were missing were his laptop and some Church files he kept in the front room upstairs. He bolted the front door and called to Mrs Lacey over the back wall. She came out, delighted to see him.

'So how was our glorious leader? Did he want to consult you on Church-state relations?'

'Kind of,' said Christopher. 'Did you hear anyone call to my house while I was away?'

'Not a dickeybird,' said Mrs Lacey. 'And I don't have to tell you I was all ears. I spent half the morning standing in my doorway, smoking, keeping watch. No one came next or near your house.'

Christopher climbed over the wall and into her yard.

'Oh, I like your jeans. Don't you look handsome? What's happening now? Have you got a date? Do you not want people to know you're a bishop?'

He looked her straight in the eye.

'I've discovered I don't believe in God any more. I intend to leave the Church.'

'Well holy Jesus, that's one for the books! Here, let me look at you.'

He stood stiffly while she looked him over.

'I'm sorry to tell you but you still look like a priest. Once a holy Joe, always a holy Joe. You never lose that look. I don't know what it is. I think it has to do with never having thought about sex without immediately saying a hundred Our Fathers and another hundred Hail Marys. God forgive me, though I don't believe in Him either.'

They went into her kitchen area. Mrs Lacey offered to make him some tea. He accepted the offer and she told him to help himself to the packet of biscuits that was lying beside the kettle.

'I haven't believed in God in years,' she said. 'I don't know if I ever did. I used to pretend when I was little, like everyone else, but I gave that up when there was no point any longer. I didn't tell you before, I don't know why. Maybe I was afraid I'd upset you, or offend you. Isn't that stupid? You're better off, as far as I'm concerned. When you think of all the hours people spend, going to mass on Sundays and saying their prayers at bedtime or whatever. Sure what harm have most of them ever done? None. Most of them would run a mile if they saw a sin. And they're all scared out of their knickers that they might go to hell. The whole thing is stupid when you think about it.'

The rucksack of documents he had given her was sitting on the floor just inside the back door. She saw him looking at it.

'I nearly broke me back lugging that in from the yard. I looked in it but I was bored before I'd read the first page. Why you would want to hide that drivel from anyone I don't know. So what did Brady want?'

Christopher told her he had done something that had upset Brady, that Brady had somehow found out, and wanted him to back off.

'Is it something to do with what's in the bag?'

'Yes.'

'Oh Jesus! This is like James Bond or something. Though I'm a bit old for Ms Moneypenny.'

When he had finished the tea, he told her he would take the bag and be on his way. She let him out her front door. He looked up and down the street to make sure there was nobody about.

'Look after yourself,' she said. 'That Brady always struck me as a nasty little bollix.'

He walked through the Basin and down to Dorset Street where he flagged a taxi and asked to be brought to Nassau Street. He went to a photocopying centre and settled in to make copies of the documents in the rucksack. One of the assistants gave him some boxes and he arranged the copies into the boxes, a full set in each box. Then he went to a computer café and wrote an extensive covering note, printed out four copies of it, and put one into each of the boxes. Then he sealed and addressed each box. He addressed one to the Revenue Commissioners, one to the Garda Fraud Bureau, one to *The Irish Times*, and one to the Catholic Archbishop of Armagh. He looked up the number for the Botanical Gardens and then used his mobile phone to call James. 'I want to ask you to do me a favour,' he said, when the young American came on the phone. Afterwards he went back to the photocopying centre, stood outside and flagged down a taxi, loaded the boxes of photocopied documents into its boot, and had the driver take him to the Botanical Gardens. He directed the taxi to the staff car park beside the gardens, where James met him and they put the four boxes in the boot of his car. Christopher gave James some money and James assured him that he would take the boxes to the post office first thing the following morning unless Christopher contacted him and told him not to.

'Thanks,' said Christopher. 'I have a meeting to go to. I'm sorry to be so mysterious about all this. It's a long story and, if you don't mind, I won't tell you what's behind it all. I need some time to think before I finally decide to send off this material, but I have a reason for not wanting to hold on to it myself at the moment. I just have to ask you to trust me.'

'Jeez,' James said. 'Any time, Christopher! Any time.'

TWENTY-THREE

CHRISTOPHER LEFT THE GARDENS and made his way to the Archbishop's Palace. Walking up the path through the trees, he thought of the dog he had thumped with the rucksack. There was no sign of blood, no evidence of the violence of the night before. The grounds were empty save for Whelan's crimson Nissan Micra, looking modest and somewhat forlorn alone in the small parking area.

Now it's my turn, Christopher thought, to be swatted.

Whelan surprised him by inviting him into the sitting room of his small, private apartment. He remained standing after telling Christopher to sit on a chair by the window. During all that followed, Whelan did not sit. He paced the room, leaned against the window frame, sat on the edge of his desk, then resumed his pacing of the room. He acted like a concerned and patient hospital consultant. The papers on Whelan's desk, Christopher knew, had to do with the upcoming Synod, but Whelan, not wearing a jacket and with the sleeves of his black shirt rolled up, appeared to have all the time in the world.

'First of all,' said Whelan. 'I want you to tell me what you are doing about these documents.'

Christopher said he had copied them and had arranged for them to be sent to the Archbishop of Armagh, *The Irish Times*, the Garda Síochána and the Revenue Commissioners. Whelan emitted a long, loud sigh that was suffused with a great sadness.

The room had two large sash windows looking out onto the pines and chestnuts. It faced east, away from the noise of traffic, and Christopher thought of how the low morning sun must stream in the windows, lighting up the blues and reds in the woven rug that covered the stained wooden floor. A representation of the Sacred Heart hung over a plain mahogany fireplace, and a picture of the Holy Father hung from the opposite wall. A statue of the Virgin, holding her child, stood on a wooden pedestal in the corner opposite where Christopher sat. There was not one personal item on display that he could see, no picture of a niece or nephew, or of Whelan's siblings or his deceased parents. But perhaps, Christopher thought, somewhere in the room was a trinket, a scarred scunger from Whelan's childhood, a sock worn by his father on his deathbed, some souvenir from the land of personal love.

'No doubt Armagh will contact you before the Synod takes place,' Christopher said.

Whelan smiled.

'In the normal scheme of things, I'd have had the documents sent to you so you could dive right in, like a child at Christmas. You could rip open the wrapping and put the toy together. Then you'd come back to me and tell me all that you'd discovered.'

An expression of affection was the last thing Christopher had been expecting.

Whelan walked to the mantelpiece, ran the fingers of one hand almost sensually over the polished wood.

'You're not just seeking attention are you? You're sure you're well?'

Christopher did not take offence. What surprised him was the sincerity of the Archbishop's concern.

'To be honest, I'm withered with the whole thing. I'm hoping one consequence of sending the documents off will be that the responsible authorities, knowing they are being watched by the media, will properly tackle the issue, and I can get on with my new life.'

Whelan didn't respond and a dark thought crossed Christopher's mind.

'And even if nothing happens, well I can still walk away feeling that I did all that I could.'

Whelan turned and leaned his large back against the mantelpiece. When he spoke his tone was conversational.

'Am I one of those responsible authorities?'

Christopher said nothing. Whelan emitted another heartfelt sigh.

'You have no idea how many people I have to consult. Lawyers, insurance people, media advisers, the Nuncio, the heads of the religious orders, politicians. Everyone looking out for their own interest. I am trying to do the Lord's work, and I have enemies everywhere.'

He walked to a window, turned a wooden chair around so he could lean on the top of the backrest. He looked intently at Christopher.

'At times I feel I am drowning in administration. These problems you are creating, from my point of view they can appear to be just more unnecessary administration. It is one of the great challenges of management: deciding what is worth focusing on, what issue will benefit the most from your time. You are being guided by principle, by what is right, but in my job I need to do more than that. I need to prioritise, chose *between* imperatives. However, that's not what I wanted to talk about today. I want to talk to you about your everlasting soul. Do you still say you no longer believe?'

Christopher returned Whelan's stare, thinking that the Archbishop could have been a film actor and have played the role of the handsome hero, the strong man everyone knows they can trust.

'I don't believe a word of it. I'm an atheist.'

'Did you believe when we were on the altar in the Pro-Cathedral and I was ordaining you a bishop of the Church?'

Christopher said he couldn't answer that question. He said it felt as if he hadn't believed in God for years. It was like trying to remember what it had been like to be a teenager. All he could say was that he did not believe in God now. Not one bit. The realisation had been sudden, but the gestation, he believed, must have been under way for some time. 'I think it was my being made a bishop that brought it to a head. It made me be more in the world, if you can understand that. And once I found myself in the world, being listened to, I found that I didn't believe. The loss of faith, when it came, was instant and complete, so much so that I find it difficult now to remember what it was like to have ever believed.'

He told Whelan that his mother had received the news with something close to gladness. That a woman in her seventies who lived next door to him had immediately confessed that she hadn't believed in God for years, perhaps never did. Faith in Ireland had lasted longer than it had in many Western Europe countries, but that was not the same as saying it was robust.

'I think you preside over a church of allegiance as much as one of faith.'

Whelan stood and walked around the room, stopped by the door, lifted a chair and placed it by a glass-doored set of bookshelves heavy with ecclesiastical tomes. He came to rest by one of the windows and spoke without turning around.

'In the western world today people want to squeeze as much pleasure and self-fulfilment as they can out of their individual lives. That seems logical to them, but it is in fact inadequate. They underestimate not just the importance of their spiritual situation, but also the power of evil. They deny the Devil. In the end the material view fails to satisfy their spiritual nature, they grow despondent, and evil flourishes. All of which places the world in grave danger.'

Christopher looked at Whelan's broad, strong back.

'Are you arguing for belief on utilitarian grounds?'

For some time the Archbishop didn't respond.

'No,' he said. 'God sent his only son into the world to suffer and to die, so as to help us find our true nature. So that we could know what it meant to live according to his plan. His son entered into history to give us guidance, and this Church is the instrument of that guidance.'

'I don't believe any of that. I just think it's nonsense.'

When Whelan turned to face the room again, Christopher was startled to see the pain on his face.

'I have been thinking,' Christopher said. 'If there is no God, then people created him, not the other way round. They created the message of Jesus; all the wisdom that exists from history. It's not necessary to despair.'

Whelan stepped quickly across the room, stopped when he was

right up against Christopher, and placed his hands on Christopher's scalp. Then, extraordinarily, he leaned down and kissed him on the top of his head. It was done with such gentleness, paternalism and such obvious love that it reminded Christopher of the concept of God's blessing.

'Once,' Christopher said, 'when I was a young man, in a wild overgrown lane down the back of the house where my mother still lives, I experienced the presence of God.'

TWENTY-FOUR

'It was a beautiful day, a spectacularly beautiful day. The month of May. I was preparing for my Leaving Cert, studying in my room, when I got the notion of going down the lane and continuing my studies there. The lane has a line of green grass and weeds running down the centre, and compacted muck ruts on each side from the wheels of neighbours' cars. Opposite the back of each house there is a lot, with the lots getting bigger the farther down the lane you go. At the end of the lane the lots are the size of small fields. In the old days they were for people to park their horses and carts in. We used to play in the lots when we were children. When we went down there we felt as if we were in the countryside, far from parental supervision. It was a land of our fantasies and dreams.

'The last lot, the McGready's, was bordered on all sides by tall trees and wild bushes. I went in through the gap in the bushes that was known to us children, found a place to sit in the long, warm grass, and I started to read my biology textbook. There was a high blue sky above me, a few scuttling pure white clouds, a silence that was enhanced by the singing of birds. "What am I?" I began asking myself, putting aside my studies. "What is life for?"

'I thought I could make some sense of the question if I listed what it was I did. I ate. I slept. I dreamed. These, it seemed to me at the time, were my major activities. I repeated the words over and over, as a sort of mantra. "I eat, I sleep, I dream. I eat, I sleep, I dream." It is easy to scoff at the young, but you have to remember the intensity with which they experience life, and how momentous the concept of the future appears to them. They are coming face to face with the almost frightening reality of free will. My sheltered youth had me feeling restless. I wanted more, more than just sleeping, eating, dreaming. And what I wanted most of all was to understand.

'I lay back on the grass and looked up at the sky and at the tops of the trees around me. The shapes of the trees, in particular, attracted my attention. Their balance and grace, the way their branches stretched out before the immensity of the sky. The beauty and peace of the scene moved me greatly, and I lay there looking at this magnificence and repeating my mantra, and a change came over me. It was an emotional but also an intellectual progression.

'I began to feel at one with everything around me, with the ground and the grass beneath me, with the warmth of the air, the air itself, the colours I could perceive. I felt that I and all that I could see and feel, and all that I couldn't see and didn't know about, were part of one enormous, eternal, inseparable whole. It was not just that I too was made from the material stuff of the universe. Everything, it seemed clear to me, pulsed with the same strong, steady sense of joy which I was then feeling. Everything was not just suffused with love, but *was* love. At its core, the substance of everything was love. In the way the physicists would tell you that everything in the universe is, in one sense, energy. But I felt this energy to be love. Unending, ceaselessly radiating, joyful love.'

Whelan stood unmoving beside him while Christopher spoke. He felt somehow certain that he was successfully conveying to the Archbishop what had happened to him that day.

'And this love was God. It came from him and it was him, and I was both of him and in his presence. I cannot overemphasise how strong and clear this epiphany was. How irrefutable and obvious was what had been revealed to me. I felt . . . we were there together, down that lane, both of us, God and I, united in an experience of love that was so strong, it was a form of ecstasy. And I thought of the Decalogue. Thou shalt not . . . Thou must . . . And it all seemed wonderfully amusing. Because why would anyone instruct you not to steal or insult God or covet the goods of your neighbour? Once you had discovered your true nature, and that of the whole universe, you had no inclination whatsoever to do any of those things. Such acts made no sense in a world of ceaseless, unending joy and love. I thought of the idea of a ladder, which you climbed to get where you wanted to go, but had no need of thereafter, and so left behind. A tool no longer needed. Such was my view of the Commandments.

'Why would anyone want to commit a bad or an evil act? To think like that was a manifestation of a lack of understanding. It was a type of immaturity or childishness, in the sense that the motivation for such acts could arise only in someone who had not discovered the true nature of existence; in someone who had not come into direct contact with God, who was real and was both the source of love and love itself. Badness, ill fortune, even what we call evil, were minor issues compared to the reality of ceaseless and unconquerable love. From the perspective of God's boundless and unceasing love, evil wasn't important.

'What I want to tell you most of all is the absolute certainty I felt on that day in the lane behind our house. It was a revelation, an encounter, and it was forceful and utterly convincing. I have never forgotten it. At the core of its power was my sense of absolute certainty.

'My father died in that lane. He was working on some rose bushes he had planted outside our back gate and he went for a stroll down to the end of the lane – we don't know why – and while he was there he was struck with a sudden heart attack. He fell to the ground close to the patch of land where I lay that day looking at the beauty of the trees and the blue May sky. I presume there was a time, a few minutes perhaps, when he lay there with excruciating pain in his chest, struggling to breathe, knowing he was likely to die. Most likely frightened. Looking up at that same blue sky, those same treetops. At a sky that I now find myself believing was oblivious of his pain, knows nothing of joy and love, loss and regret. Of grief and orphaned love.

'So what am I to think now, lying on my back in my imaginary lane, looking up at the beauty of the world? What am I to do with the certainty of that day? With the fact of my epiphany?'

TWENTY-FIVE

SIMONE CAME THROUGH THE GAP between the sliding glass doors wheeling a large black suitcase, not looking around to see if there was anyone in the arrivals lounge to meet her. She was speaking with two men wearing dark suits and pulling almost identical cases. All three looked tired and somewhat grumpy. Christopher stood back and watched them pause and exchange a last few comments. Simone nodded to both men, left them, and looked disinterestedly around. When she spotted Christopher, she made no effort to conceal her surprise and delight.

'I suppose I'd better not hug and kiss a bishop in the middle of the arrivals lounge in Dublin Airport,' she said as she leaned forward and kissed his cheek. Her perfume brought him back to the night of their dancing in her kitchen and he let his eyes make clear to her the fact of his affection.

'I get so fucking fed up of arriving back in this airport and everyone being met by someone except me,' she said.

'You look tired.'

'You wouldn't believe the few days I've had.' The skin under her eyes was dark from fatigue and her hands were shaking slightly. 'Talk about tension and high stakes. I shouldn't say it but Hogan's world is in danger of falling apart. The bankers are rattled and their exposure to him, and to the Irish market, is astronomical. If it wasn't for the Seafront Towers, we might not have a way out. But let's not talk about bankers or business or bloody property. What have you been up to?'

He told her he had also been busy.

'I'm going to leave the Church.'

Straightaway she was alert and obviously wary.

'Now hang on, Christopher. This has nothing to do with me, does it? I mean we had a great dinner together and maybe I shouldn't have let you see me to bed, but let's keep things in perspective.'

His heart sank. There was no mistaking her hostility.

'I've just had a very strange and stressful few days.'

She stood there looking cross, furious even.

'Can we go somewhere and talk?' he said.

'Look, Christopher, I barely know you, and you are laying a really big heavy on me. We talked, drank too much wine. We danced and kissed. I don't mean to offend you but in the real world that is not such a big deal. Frankly, it happens quite a lot.'

All around him parents were embracing their children, partners their partners, friends were clasping the hands of friends. A young boy with a halo of red curls leapt up on his mother and embraced her with both his arms and legs. An elderly man shyly put out his hand to welcome home his adult son. A man wearing a red football jersey walked by holding the hand of his blond, lank-haired son dressed in the same colours.

Christopher had thought he was on the cusp of joining this world, but it now appeared that he had been mistaken. The terrible thought crossed his mind that he would never understand.

'It's got nothing to do with you,' he said, forcefully. 'I never said that it did.'

She paused, wondering if she should believe him.

'Okay,' she said, not sounding very convinced.

'I'd love to tell you everything. Would you mind? Perhaps you're too tired?'

She said she needed to sleep but was probably too wired. 'Let's go and have something to eat in the airport hotel and you can tell me your story. Then I can go home and try to sleep through to tomorrow morning. Hogan's gone to New York, so he will be out of my hair until then at least.'

In the hotel restaurant they found an isolated table, ordered salads and water. Simone asked for a glass of Sancerre. A soulless, orchestral version of Debussy's *Clair de Lune* was playing quietly from almost concealed speakers. On the wall near them was a print of a hunt, strangely elongated horses easily vaulting a country hedge. The depicted scene was in sharp contrast with the view through the large plate glass window of roads and traffic and the enormous hulk of an aircraft hangar. One of the defining characteristics of the current period, Christopher thought, is dishonesty. Almost everywhere, it seemed to him, there were apartments and houses being built in places where no one wanted to live. The designation 'starter homes' was an acceptance of this by everyone involved. There were high spec hotels that looked out over noisy motorways and had air-conditioning systems that made guests feel they were sleeping in the bowels of an ocean-going ship. There were ultra-modern commercial buildings whose deterioration began before the first tenant had moved in. There were evangelical technology companies trying to tell you their products were existentially, almost spiritually, empowering, and that the profit motive had nothing to do with their production and sale. The biggest lie of all, however, was the one that everyone had suddenly become rich. Christopher often despaired when he came across media coverage of Ireland's supposed new-found wealth and its obsession with possession, when it was perfectly clear to anyone who opened their eyes while walking through the city that for most people material wealth was a stranger who would never call to their door. Society, he thought, paid a high price for acceding to dishonesty.

When the food arrived, Christopher took up Simone's invitation to tell all. He told her about meeting Mary O'Mahoney and about the house she lived in, about the wines she opened and did not drink, about her divorce arrangements, and about the documents she had given him. Simone stopped him at this point.

'Are you sure you want to tell me this?'

'I have already sent the documents to the Revenue, the Garda, the Archbishop of Armagh, and *The Irish Times*. I gave them all covering letters in which I told them who I was and my interpretation of what was in the files. I didn't say who had given them to me. I hope you won't tell anyone that she gave them to me.'

'Well, it will be pretty bloody obvious. And she might well sue you. If you're wrong in your suspicions, or unable to prove them, then you could be in serious trouble.'

It was obvious that she thought what he was doing was ill-advised, but also that she was determined not to get involved. She let him speak.

'The Church can't learn that properties it received over the years from O'Mahoney's clients were associated with tax evasion and then do nothing about it. The Church can't collude with and protect people who broke the law of the land, people who stole, leaving it to others to fund the teachers who staff the schools that the Church runs. It's shot through with hypocrisy and moral failure.'

He was, Christopher noticed, trying to justify his thoughts and actions.

'I've spent my adult life as a seminarian and then a priest. I'm hard-wired at this stage to think in terms of doing good. What is the right thing to do has always been my guiding principle. If I do nothing with these documents, that is a moral choice. If I seek to draw attention to the wrong-doing, that is a moral choice. If my suspicions are correct and my actions become public knowledge, then my choice becomes a moral example. Such is life, for everyone – an endless succession of moral choices. If you try to be good, you become good at being good. If you don't, then you don't. That sounds ridiculously simple, but it has to be true. Think about it. How could it be otherwise?'

She said nothing.

'One of the properties I have my suspicions about is the land Buzzie Hogan wants for the Seafront Towers site.'

She had been picking at her salad. Now she held her fork in mid-air and stared hard at him. For a time she was slack-jawed and silent. Then she said, 'Oh Jesus.' She dropped the fork onto her plate and rested her face in her cupped hands.

'Fuck. Fuck. Fuck. Fuck. Fuck it. Fuck. Fuck. Fuck.'

When she lifted her head, he saw she was close to tears.

'Are you saying you don't want the transfer to go ahead?' she asked.

'I can't say. I'm leaving the Church. I've told Whelan. He will have to take advice. I met him earlier today, and my guess is that the land will not be sold. Not for a while anyway. If my suspicions are correct, then I think Whelan's wish may be to confront the issues that have arisen. This whole business has presented him with the possibility of redeeming his position, if not within the Church, then in society generally. He really wants the people to be able to have faith in him, so that in turn they will have faith in the Church.'

'Just hang on,' said Simone. She lowered her face into her cupped hands again, struggling to suppress a sense of panic. She stood up and walked to the hotel lobby, paced around there for a few moments, then came back into the restaurant and sat down.

'You're not talking to me in confidence, but I want to say something in confidence to you. Agreed?'

He agreed. It was obvious that the stress she was feeling was all but overwhelming her.

'We were in London discussing the renewal of some of Hogan's banking facilities. Four hundred and fifty million pounds sterling. He has gone to New York to discuss a further four hundred and fifty million dollars. Our funders are scared shitless. If they lose their nerve, everything collapses. But if they want to keep going, they have to put more money on the table. Do you understand? The whole thing has grown so big, and the only way the banks can get out of the mess is if the Seafront Towers goes ahead, and soon. Hogan wants to sell some of the project up front, off the plans, so he can reduce his borrowings before the whole house of cards starts to totter. I shouldn't be telling you this, but I want you to understand what's going on. If Hogan falls, other property developers will too. Do you know what happens when property booms collapse, Christopher? Banks get fucked, businesses close all over the place, thousands . . . tens of thousands of people lose their jobs, their livelihoods. Enormous amounts of wealth are destroyed, lives are ruined, countries go into recession for years. You need to understand this. You need to know what you're doing.'

He was stunned. She was looking at him as if he was the enemy. Her tone had become one of condescension and disdain. She was a solicitor, trying to bully her client's adversary.

'That's bullshit, Simone. Either there was tax evasion or there wasn't. The rest is bullshit.'

It was her turn now to be surprised. He thought she might burst into tears. Her neck muscles were so tense, they were making her head shake.

'I'm just so fucking tired,' she said. 'Ask the waiter for some coffee, will you?'

When the coffee came, she cooled it with milk, drank two quick cups, said she was not going to sleep now anyway. She looked at her watch.

'I have to go. When I get home, I'm going to call Hogan. He'll probably tell O'Mahoney. You'd better be ready for whatever is coming.'

She called for the bill, stood and began to ready herself for leaving. Even her movements were angry. Christopher remained seated. He wasn't sure if this was a row or a parting of the ways.

'You know O'Mahoney is a consultant for the Seafront Towers? He lobbied the government, won himself an enormous success fee when he got Brady onside. You are making yourself some very powerful and very dangerous enemies, Christopher. These men are used to getting their way.'

He let her pay the bill and followed her out of the hotel. They walked together to the taxi rank and Christopher accepted her curt offer of a lift. The taxi driver presumed they were a couple, asked them had they been on holidays. Simone shut down his questioning with a harshness that emphasised to Christopher how little he knew about the woman he was sitting beside. The driver turned up his radio and drove towards the city in silence.

'So is this why you're resigning? Disgust?'

'No,' he said. 'It's not that at all.'

He didn't elaborate and she didn't press him. The taxi made its way slowly through the traffic-choked city. Christopher said nothing as it passed near Broadstone. Simone didn't comment either. When they came to her house, they both got out of the car and she left her front door open for him so he could walk in after her and close it behind them.

TWENTY-SIX

CHRISTOPHER SAT ON A STUFFED chair in Simone's yellow-wallpapered, chintz-curtained front room. He listened, with a sense of appreciation and relief, to the silence. Simone was upstairs taking a shower and he imagined her, this woman he hardly knew, naked under a jet of water inside glass panels, rubbing soap over her skin, her bosoms, her beautiful muscled stomach, her shanks, stepping out afterwards and rubbing her inspiring body with a soft white towel. He wondered at the force of his desire to tell her what he felt about her physical form. How he wanted to share his sense of marvel. He wondered if she, or women generally, knew of the effect their bodies could have on men's souls, of the extent to which the sight of her beautiful breasts haunted him in a way that he had come to cherish. What was strange about it, he wanted to say to her, was the mingling of intense, inner, abstract concerns, with something so physical and so, literally, of the flesh. Church history, since the time of St Augustine, had warned of the spiritual danger inherent in the lure of the female form, but here he was now, in her home, thinking of her in her shower, and so filled with the idea of the transcendent.

When she came down, she was wearing a cream nightshirt with slits at the sides, out of one of which one of her long, strong legs emerged as she turned and closed the door after her. Her hair hung wet around her shoulders. She flopped into an armchair across the room from him and fixed him with a look of determined resentment.

'I was to go to Venice with a friend in two weeks' time. I assured her last week that the Seafront Towers would be put to bed by then,

163

the banks satisfied; that there would be an opening for us to get away. She's booked the tickets, hotel room. It's a lot of money for her. And I was looking forward to it so much. To get away, pamper myself, forget about all this shit. Have some time for myself. I'm so fed up with people stealing my time.'

The difference, he thought, between sacred and profane love was the issue of certainty. You could love someone, but never be sure of them. And you would never truly know them, and they would never truly know you. But then there had been that moment in her bedroom just five days earlier. That had felt like certainty.

'Everybody I know, everyone I've worked with and encountered over the past decade, has been slaving to get some advantage for themselves; to earn some money so they can put a roof over their heads, buy things, go on holidays. What's so wrong with that? What's wrong with working for personal advantage?

'But you have to go around sticking your nose into other people's business and deciding whether you approve or disapprove, causing trouble, drawing attention to yourself like some sort of desperately insecure celebrity. People have jobs, dreams, ambitions; why can't you leave them alone? You're not the fucking police. Even *they* don't go out of their way like you do, acting on the basis of suspicions and pet theories. You said you're going to resign from the Church. Why don't you just go away and leave everyone be? Stop causing so much trouble.'

'From what you say, everything's on the verge of collapse anyway.'

She pounced like a predator.

'But you never know! That's the point. A push this way or that could make all the difference. We might just get away with it. For Hogan, it has always been a gamble. Heads I make a fortune, tails everything's fucked. The bankers are the same. Everyone's gambling, pushing things to the edge. It's the way the world works. Your interference could ruin it for everyone.'

Her hair had made dark wet patches on the shoulders of her shirt. He was so bored by what she was saying. Bored more to anger than to tears.

'Why can't you just go and do whatever it is you want to do with the rest of your life, listen to music, drink wine, whatever, and leave everyone else to get on with their lives? What's in it for you?'

He wondered if he shouldn't just walk away, but he didn't want to. Killing the dog with the rucksack full of documents had somehow changed him and he wasn't ready yet to crawl back into his cage. All his life he had been quiet, had never sought out what it was he wanted. And what he wanted now was not just to have her but also to speak his mind, to say what it was he thought. He had a chance to speak, and he was going to do so. If he lost her, then so be it. If Hogan's business empire collapsed, if banks lost hundreds of millions, well so be it. Why should he defer to their avarice? The kind of silence he had been living with was a form a death. The kind of dishonesty society lived with was a form of death. The arguments against his speaking out were all bullshit.

'From what you've said, I take it you could still get the documents back,' she said. 'Why don't you do that? Then just walk away from matters that don't concern you. Do it for me, Christopher.' She pulled her feet up under her on the chair and looked straight at him. 'Do it for me.'

He stood up.

'No, Simone. Not even for you.'

He started towards the door.

'Wait!' she said. 'Sit down. Please.'

He sat again. Simone covered her face with her hands, took a deep breath, looked up at him with an expression on her face he could not decipher. Emotional exhaustion, perhaps. A woman so able and so rich, he thought, and it has led to this.

'Have you ever been to Venice?'

Never, he told her. She slumped back into her chair and began to address the fireplace.

'There's a beautiful hotel on the Grand Canal where we stay. My friend and I had planned to ride around on the public water buses, stop in cafés whenever we wanted for coffees or spritzers; go to galleries or old palazzos; eat in expensive restaurants; sleep. There are shops in the narrow

165

streets behind Piazza San Marco where I buy clothes, beautiful shoes. I get up early in the morning to watch the men in the market organise their stalls. I like standing at the counter of a tiny café having my coffee while they shout and sing outside and stack their fruit and vegetables, lay out their huge arrays of fish. There are these lovely bars near the courts where you stand outside in your coat drinking white wine and eating minuscule sandwiches. And what I love maybe most of all about Venice is the relative silence, the absence of cars, alarms, all the noise of the modern world. When you lie in your hotel room at night, it's as quiet as if you were up some empty mountain. You can feel such peace.'

She stopped. He noticed the gentle ticking of the antique clock on the mantelpiece.

'I don't have many friends,' he said. 'John, he's a bishop. No one outside the Church. My only women friends are my neighbour, Mrs Lacey, and my mother. Both of them were born before the Second World War.'

She almost smiled.

'I envy you your ability to walk away,' she said.

'I haven't chosen to walk away. I have no choice. I no longer believe in God. It came to me the night after we had dinner here, though I think the loss of faith happened before that, maybe quite some time before.'

'You said it had nothing to do with me.'

'And I was telling the truth. It *has* nothing to do with you. Bishops are considered part of an apostolic succession. Their ordination is thought to constitute God's will. At the upcoming synod I would be required to make a profession of faith. "I believe in one God, the Father, the Almighty, maker of heaven and earth, of all that is seen and unseen. I believe in one Lord, Jesus Christ, the only Son of God, eternally begotten of the Father, God from God, Light from Light, true God from true God, begotten, not made, one in Being with the Father." And so on. When a man is ordained a bishop, the Church considers him to have jurisdiction over what is required by God for people to secure eternal salvation. All this just came to me as I was sitting in my yard, and it was suddenly so clear to me – I don't believe

I was selected by God, or that I can tell people what they have to do to earn eternal salvation. Then it came to me that not only was I not suited to be a bishop, but that I'm not suited to be a priest. Because I don't believe any more. Not just the tenets of the Christian faith and the divinity of Jesus. I don't believe in any God. It wasn't you. It was my being made a bishop that was the instrument for my loss of faith. My being made a bishop made me realise something I should have known: that my religious belief melted away a long time ago.'

She let the silence hang, sat there as if wondering if she should believe him. The freshening effect of her shower had worn off and once again she looked haggard. Simone was no longer young. Life, he thought, is such an unstoppable, relentless flow, filled with events that occur and are done with. Seen from this perspective, the chintz curtains, the expensive wallpaper, the antique rug, her collection of expensive Venetian shoes, could be considered acts of defiance, of wonderful spiritual bravery. He sat looking at her and wondered if that was the highest to which the non-believer could aspire.

When she started to speak, she did so while looking at the floor.

'I drove to Mayo once with Hogan, to Ashford Castle for a business meeting, a social thing. He insisted on driving back to Dublin afterwards, even though we had both had a lot of wine with dinner. It was well after midnight when we set out. Hogan had brought his red Lamborghini and he drove as if he had a death wish. He could have pulled in at some hotel and suggested that we stay there together, even in the same bed, but he was more interested in playing with death. He drove at a suicidal speed. I sat beside him, crying quietly, as we tore along the motorway, overtaking every vehicle we came upon, not being overtaken by any. Hogan knew I was crying. He may even have been close to tears himself. For some reason I decided I would let fate decide if I would live or die. I decided I wouldn't interfere. We got to Dublin without incident. Hogan drove the car along the quays, up Clanbrassil Steet, up to here, stopped outside my door. I got out and went in without either of us saying a word.

'The event at Ashford had been to mark the leasing to an American multinational of a substantial office building that Hogan had bought and renovated. The lease hugely increased the value of the building, which Hogan was now going to sell. It was the sort of deal he lived for, gambling, making a killing, getting a return that was beyond his wildest dreams.

'And yet there we had been, hurtling along a motorway in the middle of the night, tempting death. I could feel something like evil inside that car; something present and undeniable and really, really terrifying. I think that is why I didn't tell him to stop. I could feel the real and certain presence of evil and it made me scared, made my nerves shiver. I don't mean the evil was coming from him. More that it was coming from the awfulness of what we did, making money we didn't need, so much of it; and from the fact that, even though we had it, we were so bored, so lost, that we had to gamble with death to see if we could feel something approaching life. And I remember thinking that if I got to sleep in my own bed that night, then when I rose the next morning I would change my life while I still had time; I would walk away from it all and try to get back something I once had. I don't know what: innocence, maybe; the ability to care. But instead I woke in the morning and Hogan rang and before I knew it I was up to my tonsils in the next deal, and my chance was gone. I think that's why Hogan and I get on so well. A lot of the staff are scared of him, or in awe of the money he can bring their way, but he and I share an understanding. We know that, despite all the money he has, and that I have, that the two of us, as far as life is concerned, have failed in a way we both understand.'

Christopher told her that she should go to bed, that she looked exhausted. She said she would have to call Hogan in the morning, tell him what she had learned. 'If he doesn't know it already. You know I think he bugs my phone. I know he bugs the phones of all his competitors. And his bankers. He has his own small intelligence division. It's supposed to be a secret but I worked it out years ago. It was the only explanation for the way he seemed to know everyone's private business.'

Christopher got up and went over to her chair, leaned over to place a kiss on her damp scalp, but she snapped at him and pushed him away.

'Get away from me! You think you can walk around destroying people's worlds and pissing everyone off, and expect them to thank you for it. You're so presumptuous, and clueless, and arrogant. Just get out, will you. I don't think I ever want to see you again. Ever.'

He stood beside her chair, panicking, thinking that if only he could find the right words, he could restore the situation. She hadn't turned to look at him.

'Just get out, will you. Go away from me.'

She sat in her chair, staring at the fireplace, acting as if he was already gone.

Christopher turned and walked out to the hall, paused there in the forlorn hope that she might call him back. He stood listening and heard only his troubled and unhappy breathing. When he stepped outside her front door, and pulled it closed behind him, it felt as if he was closing a shutter on all hope of happiness. The street was empty and the sky was dark and starless. The world had never been so godforsaken and cold. He looked straight up and his soul was filled with the idea of the void.

Numbed, sorrowful unto death, he made himself begin to walk. Behind him, well down the street, someone started a car engine.

TWENTY-SEVEN

THE CAR PULLED IN ALONGSIDE Christopher at the same time as he became aware that there was someone hurrying up the pavement behind him. Then, again at the same time, he became aware of hands grabbing his shoulders as he saw that someone was opening the rear door and beginning to step out even as the car had yet to come to a halt. The hands of the man behind him grabbed Christopher and pushed him forwards and down. The man who was getting out of the car was the man Christopher had seen the day before in the black leather jacket. Now he was wearing a white t-shirt and jeans, the t-shirt tight so that it clung to the outline of the bulging, well-formed muscle on his chest and upper arms. 'Your time has come, you f-f-fucker,' he said. The man behind him was pushing Christopher and forcing him to bend down. The man in the t-shirt, even as he was finishing his sentence, leaned in and brought his right fist out from the side of his body and up into Christopher's face, so that it smacked with shocking force into Christopher's nose. Warm, salty blood spurted onto his lips, into his mouth and down onto the pavement.

The man behind him pushed his knee against Christopher's coccyx, so that Christopher fell onto the hard ground. Even as he was assessing which part of his body had hit the ground hardest, he felt a sickening sensation throughout his being as someone kicked him hard on the side of his stomach, just below his ribs. His throat tightened and he thought he might choke. The two men began to pull him to his feet again. When he stood, he was immediately hurled towards the car. They pushed him in through the open back door, thumping his forehead against the roof of the car as they did so. The blow cut through his flesh, and sticky warm blood began to cover his eyes. The men put him lying on the floor of the car and climbed in over him. They sat on the back seat and used their feet to keep him from rising. Doors slammed and the car began to drive away at speed.

One of the men raised his foot and pressed it down hard on the side of Christopher's head. 'You're bleeding on the floor of my fucking car, you cunt,' he said. 'You're going to pay for that.' All Christopher could see was the underneath of the driver's seat and, beyond that, his feet as he worked the car's pedals. The man was wearing thick-soled shoes, the sort known as brothel creepers.

Christopher was sore in a way he had never been before. The blood that was seeping from his nose was creating a puddle on the floor around his cheek. He couldn't breathe through his nose and he wondered if it was broken. His hair felt wet and he imagined the pool of drying, sticky blood that had come from the cut on his forehead. The greatest pain was in his side where the kick he had received had thumped through to his stomach. It felt as if something watery was accumulating inside him, perhaps an internal bleed.

The car slowed as it came to the end of a street, turned left, then began to travel at greater speed. Christopher felt it stop at what he thought must be the junction of the South Circular Road and Clanbrassil Street. Soon afterwards he felt what he thought was the car rising over the hump-backed bridge that crossed the Grand Canal. After that, though, he got confused. The car travelled some distance before its next turn. It then made three or four rapid turns so that, when it started to drive steadily again, he had no idea what direction they were taking. Someone, possibly all three occupants of the car, started to smoke, and Christopher felt even more nauseous than he had been before. Warm cigarette ash fell onto his face and mingled with the blood on the floor. The acid taste of stomach juice migrated up his oesophagus. The car drove through the night-time city and he concentrated on not getting sick. He feared that if he did, the men in the car might take it as an excuse to cause him further pain.

No one spoke. The driver switched on the radio and Christopher heard the rapid-fire words of a rap song, some singer recounting the poverty of the neighbourhood where he had been raised. Then there was another, inane song, the singer repeating the verse again and again, some self-pitying lyric about wanting to be loved. The next song had one of those electronic beats that Christopher had often noticed coming from cars. Sometimes, sitting in his mother's front room, he would hear the thump, thump, thump of the beat from a car music system before he would hear the car's engine coming up the hill. Now he was inside one such car, the beat reminding him of his heartbeat, and adding to his sense of anxiety. Who were these men and what did they want with him? He didn't dare ask.

After some time he began to suspect that they were travelling uphill. Once he felt the car slow and turn sharply, as if it was rounding a steep bend. Later again he felt something odd with the pressure in his ears, though he wasn't sure if this might not have been owing to the blows to the head he had so recently received. The bleeding from his nose and the cut on his forehead had ceased, and the pool of blood his head was being pressed into had grown cold. The foot that was pressing on his head stayed where it was. At times other feet rested on his shoulders, his sides, his legs. Everyone was being patient.

When at last the car stopped, it was somewhere far from streetlights or any other form of illumination. The men quickly got out of the car and one of them reached back in to pull Christopher out by his hair, holding his head so it was towards the ground. He felt hands searching his pockets, taking his keys and phone and wallet from his trousers, and the disc containing the data given to him by Mary O'Mahoney from the inside pocket of his jacket. The ground at his feet was dry, packed dirt, covered with what he thought were pine needles and other forest flotsam. Then a black scarf was hanging beside his head and he knew that they were going to blindfold him. When the scarf pressed against the bridge of his broken nose, he felt such excruciating pain that he screamed and his knees buckled. He screamed and screamed. 'You fucking bollix!' the men shouted, and they kicked him in the stomach and neck so that he again felt he was about to choke. He lay on the ground, fighting for breath, forcing himself to remain silent. The sense of fear was overwhelming. A knee was pressed against his cheek. 'Listen, fucker,' the man told him, in a cold, informative voice. 'You try that again and we'll cut your tongue out. Don't think we wouldn't. You'd be dead wrong. We'd fucking enjoy it.'

Somehow Christopher found the strength to speak. 'Sorry,' he said. 'Sorry. It was the pain. I think my nose is broken.' The man told him that more than his nose would be broken by the time they were finished with him. 'Why?' he asked before he could stop himself. His question came out as a type of animalistic cry, its tone conveying more than the word spoken. The man who was pressing his head into the dirt with his knee leaned down close to Christopher. 'Because', he said, 'we don't like you.'

They put the scarf over his eyes, more carefully this time, then pulled him onto his feet, and forced him to walk. One man stood on each side of him, holding him by his upper arms, guiding him roughly while also ensuring that there was no possibility of escape. Once again they travelled in silence. Christopher's nose and forehead had started to bleed again and he could feel the viscous liquid seep over his lips and inside his open, torn shirt and onto the skin of his chest. Each step caused a sharp pain in his side where he had earlier been kicked. Perhaps, he thought, I have a broken rib. Or something inside me is ruptured.

He was close to claiming he could walk no farther when he was told to stop. They put him sitting on the ground, his back resting against the trunk of a tree. He sat as still as he could, breathing through his mouth, tears flowing onto his cheeks to mingle with the blood. He held his head back and after a time the blood stopped flowing from his nose. His nostrils felt as if they had been stuffed with cotton wool. Any twitch of the muscle near his nose made the bones grate. He sat as still as he could and waited. He thought he could hear them pulling on their cigarettes, and blowing the smoke out with low moans of pleasure, though he was unsure. The sound of his blood travelling through his body was oddly loud and violent. It pumped its way past his eardrums and through whatever rupture they had caused in his side. What he wanted most in the world was to be allowed lie down, and to not move; to concentrate on not moving, and to take comfort from his tears.

'What do you want from me?' he said, after they had sat for some time in silence.

'Nothing,' said a man a few feet directly in front of where Christopher was sitting.

'Job s-s-satisfaction.'

They all laughed at this.

'That's right,' said another man, somewhere to Christopher's left. 'We just want to hone our skills. See if we're still up to it.'

They all laughed a little, and then they let the silence settle. One of the men told Christopher to stop his moaning. He hadn't known that he had been moaning, so he tried not to. An occasional breeze rustled the branches overhead. The men sat with admirable patience, as if what they wanted most in the world was rest.

The end of the interlude was announced by an electronic sound, a double plop like a stone landing and bouncing once on the surface of a still lake. Someone had received a text message.

'We can g-g-go ahead,' the stutterer said. 'Everything's Oxo.'

'They have them?'

'Yeah. They brought the car to the N-n-n-aul, b-b-burned it. One of the packages was addressed to th-th-the pigs. He's a f-f-fucking snitch.'

'A fucking informer.'

'The lowest of the low.'

The men were standing, coming towards him. Christopher could see over the top of the scarf but all he could see was darkness. They had known all along about the documents. He felt so enormously forsaken.

'A fucking grass. A rat,' one of them said. 'I'm going to enjoy this.'

'Do you know what?'

Christopher felt a small kick against his thigh.

'I'm t-t-t-talking to you.'

'Sorry! Sorry. What?'

'You've been a fucking p-p-pain in the ass.'

'And you're after bleeding all over the good car.'

There was something terrifying about their obvious sense of anticipation. Christopher's heart, already thumping violently, began to race so fast that he feared it would burst.

'And you're a fucking squealer. A tout in a Roman collar.'

They laughed again at that. Someone reached down, took hold of Christopher's nose and bent it to one side. The pain was of an intensity Christopher had never experienced before. He screamed and fell, wriggling on the ground like a pinned worm.

'Scream all you like. Maybe a fox will come running to help you.'

They took the scarf off his head and he could see their shapes around him in the gloom. Each of the men was standing inches from where he was lying and he knew they had only begun.

'Please. Oh Jesus, please, don't hit me again. Please.'

'Fuck off!'

One of them kicked him hard in the stomach. When he pulled his knees up to his chest, a man behind him kicked him between the legs.

'Stand up, you cunt.'

They pulled him up and put him resting against a tree. He saw the glint of a knife in one man's hand, felt the blade cut him on the stomach as the man used it to rip through his top, the shreds of which were then pulled from him. The man took off Christopher's belt and pulled his pants down so they lay around his feet. He looped the belt around Christopher's neck and tightened it so that for a moment Christopher felt the end was at hand. Then the man eased the pressure, though he left the belt there.

'Reckon he likes a bit of rough, what do you think, lads?'

They were enjoying themselves. He was sobbing, snot and blood and tears all mixing on his face.

'Maybe we should cut his prick off. Bishops don't need them.'

Christopher whimpered like a dog. He was so terrified, so willing to do whatever it would take to make what was happening end.

They put the scarf under his arms and tied it to the tree. One of the men kicked him hard on the knee so that Christopher's legs buckled beneath him. The scarf prevented him from falling to the ground.

Then the men began to take turns punching and kicking him. Eventually the scarf opened or broke and Christopher fell forward onto the ground. Even as he landed, they continued to kick him. One of the men was laughing with the untroubled happiness of a gleeful child. Christopher's whole body was in agony, though the sharp, targeted pain from his broken nose continued to make itself felt over and above his other agonies. One of the men placed Christopher's right hand over a rounded stone and then slammed a rock onto it with force. Christopher was crying uncontrollably. He could feel the broken bones inside his swelling hand. The men paused to draw breath. One of them noisily worked up a mouthful of phlegm and spat upon him.

'Let's tie him back up against the tree. See who can knock him out.'

They dragged him to his feet and pressed him against the tree trunk. He was now dressed only in his underpants. They tied his arms to some low branches using the scarf and belt to do so. He found it hard to stand and the weight of his body on his shoulders and the upper parts of his outstretched arms added to his misery.

'I'll go first,' one of the men said, taking up position. He rubbed his fist in the palm of his open left hand, drew his arm back, and punched Christopher as hard as he could. The punch landed on Christopher's jaw, causing his teeth to crunch together and more blood to spurt from his lips. Christopher had never known such pain, such weariness, and such despair.

'Fucker's still whinging.'

A second shape came and stood before him, legs akimbo. The man had his right fist nestled in his left hand, but was otherwise a blur to Christopher, whose eyes were filled with blood and tears.

'Let's see if I can shut him up.'

Christopher thought the man was weighing something heavy in his right hand. The blow hit him on the lower jaw, crunching the bone and knocking Christopher's head back against the tree trunk. For a moment he lost consciousness and when he came to, he realised his legs had buckled. He had bitten his tongue and his mouth was full of blood. He could feel loose flesh in his mouth and bits of broken tooth. His lower jaw was knocked to one side. The way his body was hanging from his tied arms made it hard for him to breathe.

A third man took up position in front of him.

'It's easy now,' one of his colleagues complained. 'He's half-gone already.'

'You guys made a m-m-mistake,' the man said, rubbing his fist just as the other two men had. 'You should have aimed for the n-n-nose. There's loads of n-n-nerves in the nose.'

The blow was accurate and forceful. There was no distinction between the intensity and sharpness of the pain, the crunching sound that signalled to Christopher the extent of the damage done, and the unexpected white light that burst before his eyes. When the blinding light faded, all Christopher could see was blackness and all he could feel was pain. Someone thumped or kicked him but he was losing consciousness and it was with a sense of both gratitude and grief that he sank into a warm black pool from which he was certain he would never emerge.

It is, he thought, finished.

TWENTY-EIGHT

EVERYTHING THEREAFTER HAD THE quality of a dream. Christopher found himself in a place of light, an intense dispersed white light that created no shadow. He was lying on clean, creaseless white cloth but he could not feel the weight of his body and it was as if he was floating in warm, dry, Levantine air. Below him was an expanse of rich meadow bordered by high, full-grown trees. High above him he could see a Marian blue sky, devoid of wind or cloud or other blemish. The stillness was undisturbed and ever would be. The silence was a balm to his soul.

Maidens came and ministered to him. The first had the straightest of hair, cut short to frame her young sallow-skinned face. She had high cheekbones and eyes that were knowing and grey. She leaned over him while she worked and he thought of a wolf, benevolent, smelling of springtime, strong and well and sent by the Lord to protect the weak. She washed his skin with a warm wet cloth, wrapped him in fresh raiment, left him as clean and fresh as the white robes she wore, the pillows on which she gently laid his head. He said not a word, watched all that happened to him. He was swathed in God's grace.

Another maiden liked to talk as she touched him, spoke of the morning, his pallor, the movement of his eyes. She named the parts of his body as she shifted them, one, then the other, then the next. She spoke a litany of the physical world as she busied herself around him and gave no thought to the idea that he might respond. She knew his name, said it to him as she combed the hair on his head, shaved his chin, clipped the nails on his fingers and toes. There, she said, her cheeks rose-coloured from her efforts, the heave of her chest accompanying her words. There.

Another was given to harsh-sounding or even callous phrases, though he knew her to be even more wise and gentle than the others. Her sureness of touch had the nature of a blessing. She too had her hair cut short like a boy's and wore make-up that drew attention to her moving lips. He watched her speak to others beyond his view while she busied herself with him, knowing that she knew not just his every need but every desire, and frowned at none. Sometimes she brought others to see him, all dressed in bright, stainless white, and they stood over him and spoke of him and marvelled at what they saw. One day soon, she said, he will come back to us, dwell again in the land of the living.

The light and the azure sky reminded him of the day in the lane when he had felt the irrefutable presence of the Lord. He recalled lying on his back on the warm trampled grass, looking up at the high blue his father must have watched on the day when he learned of his coming end. He imagined his father mastering his anxiety and his fear, saw himself there with him at that time, at one with him in the understanding that human life is finite, that all things end, that it is possible, even then, to be glad.

One day he opened his eyes to find his mother's fragile fingers tracing the ridges of his brow. Through her parchment skin he could feel the working of her old bones. He watched her as she struggled to arrange her old radio on the small dresser by his bed. When she turned it on, the station was playing sacred music, the shockingly beautiful sound of a choir.

Others came too – black-suited priests, bishops and nuns, blessing him and wishing him well. The radiating energy of John, in search of a purpose, the solemn power of Archbishop Whelan, focused on the burden of duty. Christopher lay in the Levantine light and Dr Reilly sat on a chair next to him, fingering his rosary beads. Hours passed in wordless communion.

The one with the grey eyes was ministering to him when he noted a familiar scent and knew Simone had come. She lowered her sad-eyed face over his, kissed him gently on the forehead, let her straw-blonde tresses for a moment fall around him and draw him back to the rich, and until then distant, world of the physical. The urge to speak was strong but he could not do so. She held one of his hands in hers, told him how sorry she was about what had happened to him, kept talking, though there was no need.

Do not trouble yourself, he wanted to tell her. None of this matters. When love is strong enough, evil is but a chimera.

TWENTY-NINE

LATE ONE EVENING JOHN CAME. Christopher, who had been sleeping, was awoken by the sound of a chair being placed by his side. His friend was dressed for cycling, wearing a high visibility yellow t-shirt and shiny black lycra shorts.

Even dressed like that, thought Christopher, he looks like a virgin.

He wished he could have said this.

'I doubted I would see you alive again,' John said with great solemnity.

Ever so gently his friend placed a hand on Christopher's side. Christopher struggled to move. The activity made his breath quicken, caused sharp pains in his ribs and chest muscles.

'You rest and I'll bring you up to speed,' John said. 'For once in your life you won't be able to interrupt.'

He told Christopher what had happened. A couple out walking in the woods had let their large Alsatian off the leash. The dog had run into the trees and came across Christopher and his assailants. It had attacked the men, who fled. Attracted by the sound of their dog's snarls and barking, the couple had found Christopher, tied to a tree by his outstretched arms, covered in blood, unconscious, the dog standing guard beside him. They had called the police.

'You were saved by a dog,' John told him smiling.

Christopher couldn't smile. His mouth was inside a metal harness that prevented him from moving his jaws.

'Do you want to hear the gossip?'

Christopher tried to nod.

What had happened had caused a national outrage. Christopher had become a celebrity. There had been hourly bulletins on his medical condition, and wall to wall media debate about his career in the Church, his good works, and how it was that such a man could be beaten almost to death.

The government had discussed the kidnapping and assault in cabinet. Brady had made a long, state of the nation speech in the Dáil which was carried live on television. It was, he had said, a stain on Ireland's character that a man as good as Christopher, a leading light of the Church, could be abducted at random and beaten to a pulp by nameless, mindless thugs. The government, he had told the people, had instructed the Garda Síochána to spare no expense in its efforts to track down the perpetrators of the vile crime. There would be no difficulty in relation to resources. New legislation, if required, would be quickly passed. The perpetrators, when caught, would face the full rigour of the law.

The Garda Commissioner had held a press conference in which he said that the men who had abducted and assaulted Christopher had intended to kill him. He said a special team of experienced detectives had been established to investigate the crime, and that he himself was taking direct charge. The President had broadcast a prime-time statement in which she spoke of the need for national moral renewal. Prosperity, she said, had caused the Irish people to lose sight of what was important in life, and to abandon the values that had been celebrated by all institutional religions over the previous two millennia.

The nation had become consumed with the idea that this random, violent attack on such a good and innocent man was symptomatic of a profound spiritual malaise. Even the dog that had saved Christopher had become a national hero. Masses were held so people could pray for Christopher's recovery, prompting Church attendances that had not been seen in decades. Whelan had held a special mass in the Pro-Cathedral which was televised live. Brady had attended with his wife and children. What had happened to Christopher had touched some profound need or worry in the contemporary psyche, John said. It had the potential to be the catalyst for a process of spiritual renewal.

News of what had happened had even spread to other countries. Christopher's image had been carried on television programmes and in newspapers on all five continents. The Holy Father had given an interview to Irish newspaper journalists in which he spoke of his shock that such a thing could happen in Ireland and after which reports of how upset he had become during the interview had been published around the globe: 'The attack on you has become linked with the sudden, ominous changes in the economy. There is widespread talk that there could be a fall, even a sharp fall, in the price of property, with grave consequences. Some are casting it as a form of retribution for society's hubris, a punishment for having turned away from God and towards materialism and Mammon. The attack on you has become mixed up in all this, and has given it a focus.'

John leaned in close. He said Whelan had told him of Christopher's apparent loss of faith, but the Archdiocese had not mentioned anything about it in public. They were hoping that it was just a temporary lapse.

'The media is treating the story as if you're the nearest thing we've had to a Messiah in two millennia. You're a kind of holy man now.'

He spoke so softly, Christopher had to strain to hear him.

'And that's got everyone worried.'

Archbishop Whelan and Dr Reilly had been having lengthy meetings in the Archbishop's Palace, he said. One of the meetings had been attended by the Nuncio.

'I'm not sure what's going on, but I gather they're worried to death about what to do if you persist in saying you no longer believe. Now that you have such a strong leadership position in the spiritual life of the nation, you've become a threat to the faith. There aren't many people who wish that dog had let those men beat you to death, but I'd say there are times when Whelan, Reilly and the Nuncio are among them.'

John looked lovingly at his friend.

'So it's just as well, from the point of view of the Church, that you can't speak.'

THIRTY

On a Saturday evening Christopher awoke to see the Archbishop standing before him. Whelan's frown was a mixture of worry and reflection. When he saw that Christopher was watching him, he assumed his usual blank look of authority and stepped forward to speak.

'You're getting better, I hear. I'm glad.'

His concern was undoubtedly genuine. He sat on Christopher's bed, made as if to touch him but then arrested the movement. Christopher thought of how odd it was that his apostasy had resulted in increased mutual respect between him and Whelan.

'We've all been very worried about you. The whole of the Catholic community has been praying for you.'

Christopher did not react in any way.

'Though as I understand your current position, you believe our prayers are addressing thin air.'

Whelan waited but Christopher was incapable of responding.

'I wanted to tell you something. It will be announced in the churches tomorrow, however I thought you deserved to hear it from me.'

There were no medical staff in the room. The television was silent. The bones of his face were paining him. Christopher thought he would wait until the Archbishop left before administering himself more morphine.

'I am to be appointed a cardinal and I will be moving to Rome. The world will be told it is an elevation, a great honour, but in truth it is a way of getting rid of me. And it's all your doing.'

Whelan looked to make sure no one else in the room was listening. He leaned in towards Christopher.

'I never heard anything from Armagh about those documents you said you'd sent them. I raised the matter, discreetly of course, with the Archbishop. He said he didn't know what I was talking about. I quizzed him a bit and I think he took offence. Later I telephoned him and told him a bit of what you had said to me. He said it wasn't our function to probe such matters. "We are the apostolic Church," he said. "We're not the FBI." '

Whelan paused, so Christopher could consider that comment.

'I dropped the matter, but afterwards I felt troubled.'

He paused again.

'It is a question, I suppose, of where you draw the line.'

Whelan closed his eyes and leaned his head back slightly. Christopher thought of how the whole episode had caused so much difficulty for so many people. Perhaps he had been too zealous.

Whelan broke the silence by quoting scripture.

'Think not that I am come to send peace on earth: I came not to send peace, but a sword. For I am come to set a man at variance against his father, and the daughter against her mother, and the daughter-in-law against her mother-in-law. And a man's foes shall be they of his own household.'

Neither of them spoke for a time. Christopher looked at the high ceiling and thought of the richness of the tradition he was leaving.

'Of course you don't believe any of that any more.'

It pained Christopher that he could not reply. But then Whelan surprised him a second time, by seemingly responding to Christopher's unspoken objection.

'For you, the words of the Son of God are reduced to just the moral insight of another human.'

Christopher wanted to say that religious belief was an expression of certain fundamental human needs. It reflected the impulse towards moral striving, and the inherent understanding in man of the importance, for the collective, and for the individual, of moral behaviour. It was a response to fear, a response to beauty; a search for meaning.

'Without God, our lives have no meaning,' the Archbishop said.

Christopher did all he could to indicate that he appreciated Whelan's comments. He so wanted to tell Whelan of the idea he had that it might have something to do with grammar, with the human requirement that a sentence should make sense. Because we have an innate capacity for grammar, he wanted to say, we have a mind that aches for completion, for resolution. For redemption.

It crossed his mind then that the same applied to music. The incessant musical logic of Bach. The inner workings of fugue and contrapuntal singing. The scales and the arpeggios his mother's students had spent so many hours practising. If music came closest to expressing the human spirit, perhaps this was simply because, like the human spirit, it was subject to the omnipresent commandments of grammar.

'And where will you get your meaning now?' Whelan said, letting one of his hands come to rest on Christopher's arm.

There was no mistaking the tone. It was an expression of genuine concern.

Christopher wanted to say he would get his meaning exactly where Whelan got his. He would create it from the materials he had been given to work with. The difference, he thought, is that he will be aware of what it is he is doing, while Whelan will be operating according to beliefs and traditions that are based on a false premise.

The older man lifted his hand from Christopher's arm and let both his hands lie limp on his lap. A nurse came to the end of Christopher's bed, checked his chart, smiled, and walked away again. The ward was quiet. The man who had been in the bed near the door and who had spent so much time listening to the television, had gone to the operating theatre some days before, and had not returned. That morning the two old men opposite Christopher had gone home. Their beds lay cleaned, tidied and empty. The whole hospital seemed suffused with the idea of waiting.

Then Whelan began to speak again.

THIRTY-ONE

'THE ARCHBISHOP'S COMMENTS WERE not the end of the matter. I decided to make enquiries about some of the bequests that you mentioned to me. I spoke with O'Mahoney. He denied everything. He demanded to know what had prompted my questioning of him, but I didn't tell him. I asked our lawyers to examine the Seafront Towers lands, to give me a paper on the matter, on the tax issues, and on our obligations. They in turn, I think, told Dr Reilly. Or perhaps it was O'Mahoney. Who knows? Dr Reilly raised it with me. I have been a bishop and an archbishop for a long time, Christopher. I recognised Dr Reilly's desire that I refrain from what I was doing. Normally that would be enough. I would submit, let the matter fade. But this time I did something different. I argued with Reilly, tried to convince him that we should, this time, try to do what was right. It is extraordinary, is it not, that you could say such a thing to a senior member of the Church, and not have him take offence? But he didn't take offence. No. He just shut me out. I could almost see the doors closing, hear the bolt being pushed home. Within days it was clear to me from the brief interactions I had with others in the palace, from a brief word I had with the Nuncio, who called on me one day, entirely out of the blue – that my role in the archdiocese had been taken from me. I was still in position, but it had become a fiction. I had no authority any more. I was yesterday's man.

'People began to behave differently towards me. If they were attentive or polite, or anxious to implement my instructions, they did so, at least in part, because they wanted to be kind.'

An element of indignation had crept into Whelan's narrative.

'I am sorry to admit that this upset me very much. I have been treated with respect, and an element of fear, for much of my adult life. Overnight that has disappeared.'

On the corridor some nurses and hospital orderlies passed, talking loudly, laughing at the story one of them was recounting. 'Thirty euro!' a man said in faux outrage. 'I told them where to shove it. "Are you mad?" I said . . ." ' The voices and the giggles faded as the happy group walked away from the door to Christopher's ward. Whelan seemed not to have noticed them or their carefree banter.

'And then I was informed that the Holy Father wants me to come to Rome. There is a position there that has to be filled, and the Nuncio has recommended me. The move will be announced from the pulpits tomorrow. The people will be told what a great honour it is for me and for the city.

'You and your actions stirred up something in my soul, and now I am no longer a trusted member of the Church.'

THIRTY-TWO

WHEN THE DAY CAME, IT WAS Simone who brought Christopher home from the hospital. His mother met him at her door, leaning on her stick. He was struck once again by how badly what had happened to him had weakened her. Soon, he thought. Very soon.

The two women walked with him into the sitting room where he was placed on the sofa in the bay window. Simone went to the kitchen and returned with a tray laden with a teapot and crockery and some biscuits. She sat beside him on the sofa and ignored the sounds he made as he drank his tea through a straw. While the women spoke of how well he was, Christopher thought of how kind Simone was being to him and of how friendly she was with his mother. He felt he was entitled to draw certain conclusions from the extent to which she had become involved in his life while he had been in hospital. She had helped his mother draw up a new will, leaving her house to him. She had put new sheets and a duvet cover on the bed in his old room to prepare for his homecoming. She had called his mother regularly on the phone to ensure that she was not wanting for anything. Between his losing consciousness in the dark woods and coming back to consciousness in the light-filled ward of the Bon Secours Hospital, Simone had somehow become a fixture in his mother's days.

His jaw had yet to heal but his arms and hands were improved to the extent that he could hold a book and read. That night when Simone had left and his mother had gone to bed, he sat in the front room beside a lamp and read some more of the book Simone had bought him when he was still in hospital. It was a new history of

Jerusalem and he stayed up late reading about the succession of tribes, religions and armies which had left their mark on the city, the monstrous crimes committed there in the name of successive gods, the horror of the cruelties the city had seen over the centuries; the way in which the bloodiness and violence of Christ's agony and death were of a piece with Jerusalem's history.

And so a few days later, when his mother asked him over breakfast if he had any thoughts as to what he might do with his future, he scribbled some words in the notebook he now carried with him.

'I want to see Jerusalem.'

She asked him if he was serious and when he convinced her that he was, she sat back and looked at him.

'You've always been a queer hawk,' she said, with her trademark mixture of scoffing and affection.

On the morning he was to travel, he woke in his old room and sat on the end of the bed looking out at the overgrown lane and the sun rising away to the east. The sight of the trees against the morning sky gave him pleasure, as it had always done, but he noted also the discarded fridges and other junk with which the lane was littered these days. A property company had bought three houses up the terrace during the boom and had converted them into multiple, one-room flats. Since then, the lots up the lane had been used to dump rubbish that the council would otherwise have had to be paid to take away. Christopher wondered if the idyllic, almost pastoral, laneway of his childhood had ever really existed.

Some day, he thought, when he was stronger, he would hire a skip and clear out the rubbish and plant the lane with fruit trees, raspberry bushes and roses.

Simone drove him to the airport. In the car they listened to guests on Nolan's radio show discuss the crisis that had hit the property market. Values had not only stalled but were beginning to fall. Sales were drying up and the banks were getting increasingly worried. Simone had already told Christopher of the delay in the closure of the contracts on the Seafront Towers, and of how, while he was in intensive care, the foreign banks had decided to withdraw from the project, and the domestic banks had quickly followed suit. On the radio they were discussing how Hogan had initiated a suite of legal cases where he was suing the banks for breach of contract.

'Winning the cases is all that stands between him and destitution,' Simone said.

Christopher responded with the throaty 'humph!', the only sound he could make with his still wired jaw.

She laughed.

'You're so cynical. Actually, he has money stashed in bank accounts around the globe. In all sorts of weird and wonderful places. You wouldn't believe it.'

They were approaching the roundabout built over the M50 just north of Ballymun. Simone was reaching forward to turn off the radio when the lights changed and she used her hands instead to hold the steering wheel and change gear. On the far side of the motorway she kept both hands on the steering wheel as they made their way up what had once been a narrow, winding country road.

Nolan announced his next guest, the religious affairs correspondent of *The Irish Times*, with whom, he said, he was going to discuss the continuing effects on the Catholic Church of the as yet unsolved crime that had been Christopher's abduction and assault.

'Already we have had the announcement that Archbishop Whelan is being created a cardinal and moving to Rome. And now we have the news that Bishop Christopher, who is still struggling to recover from the effects of the savage assault, is to retire, apparently because he is no longer capable of fulfilling the duties of that role.'

They had turned to the right and were driving on another former country lane, this time one that ran alongside the airport. On the far side of a high wire fence Christopher could see a plane coming in to land on the runway that ran parallel to the road. It was a beautiful, clear-skied day. He would fly to London, and then Tel Aviv, and that evening he would book into his room in Jerusalem. He would sleep in the city Jesus entered two millennia earlier, on the eve of the Passover, and where he held his Last Supper with his disciples. On his first morning in the city Christopher planned to go to the Garden of Gethsemane, just to sit.

As they pulled up in the short-stay car park, Nolan and his guest were still discussing the affairs of the Dublin Archdiocese. Simone turned off the car engine and sat staring straight ahead, the radio still playing.

'I wish you could talk to them.'

He shrugged. He took his moleskin notebook from his pocket and scribbled some words.

'Finished with all that.'

He was allocated a window seat. The airplane taxied to the runway, came to a rest alongside the road Simone and he had driven along an hour earlier. He had set out to expose tax evasion, had failed, and had almost been killed. But maybe, just maybe, he had ended up finding love.

What moral lesson, he wondered, could anyone draw from that?

He took a magazine from the back of the seat in front of him and flicked through articles and advertisements concerning holidays, hotels, telecoms services, watches, perfumes, airlines, alcoholic drinks, shoes.

The contemporary world, he thought, is so full of bullshit.

Despite the metal frame on his broken jaw, there was a smile on his face as the aircraft began its run. The machine lurched and he felt how the air beneath the wings lifted the plane from the earth below.

Christopher and his fellow passengers began their ascent towards the heavens.